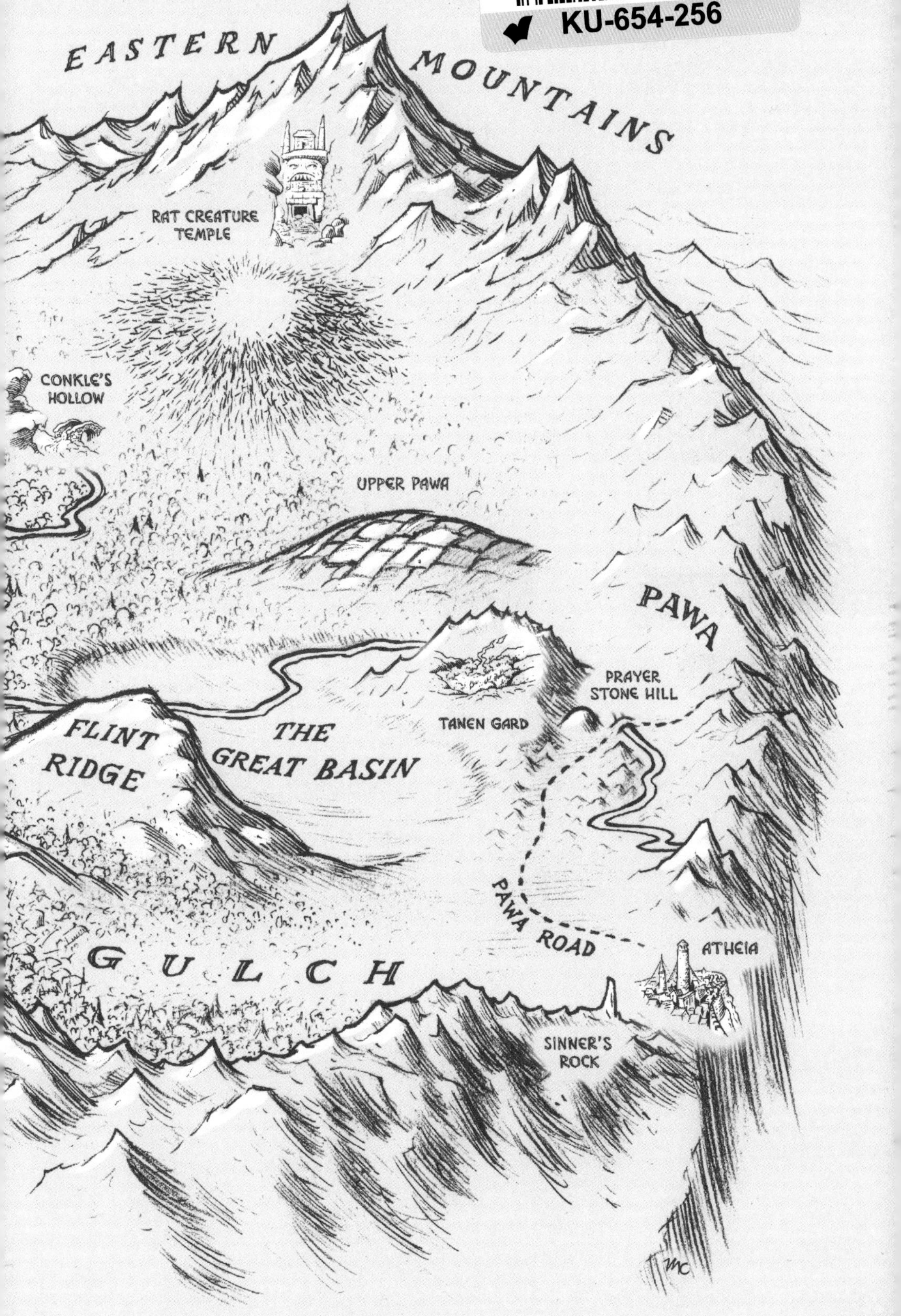
EASTERN MOUNTAINS
RAT CREATURE TEMPLE
CONKLE'S HOLLOW
UPPER PAWA
PAWA
PRAYER STONE HILL
TANEN GARD
FLINT RIDGE
THE GREAT BASIN
PAWA ROAD
ATHEIA
GULCH
SINNER'S ROCK

Dreaming of Harvestar

THE GREAT COW RACE

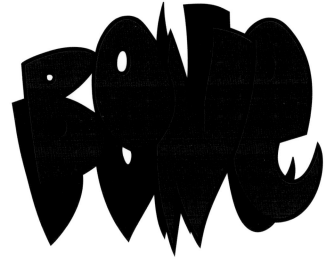

THE GREAT COW RACE

BY JEFF SMITH

WITH COLOR BY STEVE HAMAKER

An Imprint of

■SCHOLASTIC

New York   Toronto   London   Auckland   Sydney   Mexico City   New Delhi   Hong Kong   Buenos Aires

All rights reserved. Published by Graphix, an imprint of Scholastic Inc., *Publishers since 1920*. SCHOLASTIC, GRAPHIX, and associated logos are trademarks and/or registered trademarks of Scholastic Inc.

Library of Congress Cataloging-in-Publication Data available.
ISBN-13: 978-0-439-70624-7 — ISBN-10: 0-439-70624-6 (hardcover)
ISBN-13: 978-0-439-70639-1 — ISBN-10: 0-439-70639-4 (paperback)

ACKNOWLEDGMENTS
Harvestar Family Crest designed by Charles Vess
Map of *The Valley* by Mark Crilley

12 11 10 9 8 7 6 5 4 3   7 8 9 10 11 12/0
First Scholastic printing, August 2005
Book design by David Saylor
Printed in Singapore 46

This book is for Dan Root

CONTENTS

CHAPTER ONE THE SPRING FAIR

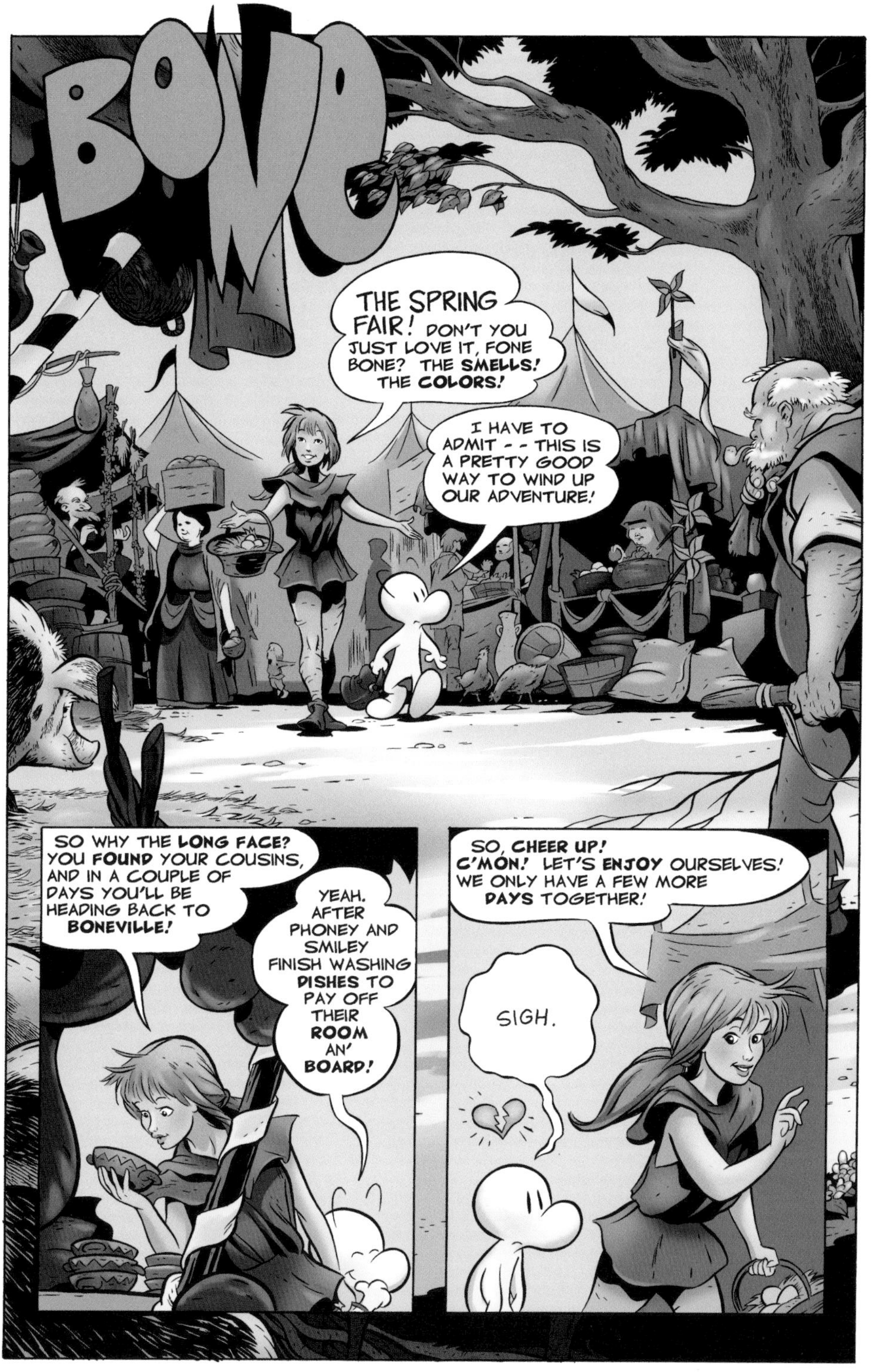
BONE
THE SPRING FAIR! DON'T YOU JUST LOVE IT, FONE BONE? THE SMELLS! THE COLORS!
I HAVE TO ADMIT - - THIS IS A PRETTY GOOD WAY TO WIND UP OUR ADVENTURE!
SO WHY THE LONG FACE? YOU FOUND YOUR COUSINS, AND IN A COUPLE OF DAYS YOU'LL BE HEADING BACK TO BONEVILLE!
YEAH. AFTER PHONEY AND SMILEY FINISH WASHING DISHES TO PAY OFF THEIR ROOM AN' BOARD!
SO, CHEER UP! C'MON! LET'S ENJOY OURSELVES! WE ONLY HAVE A FEW MORE DAYS TOGETHER!
SIGH.

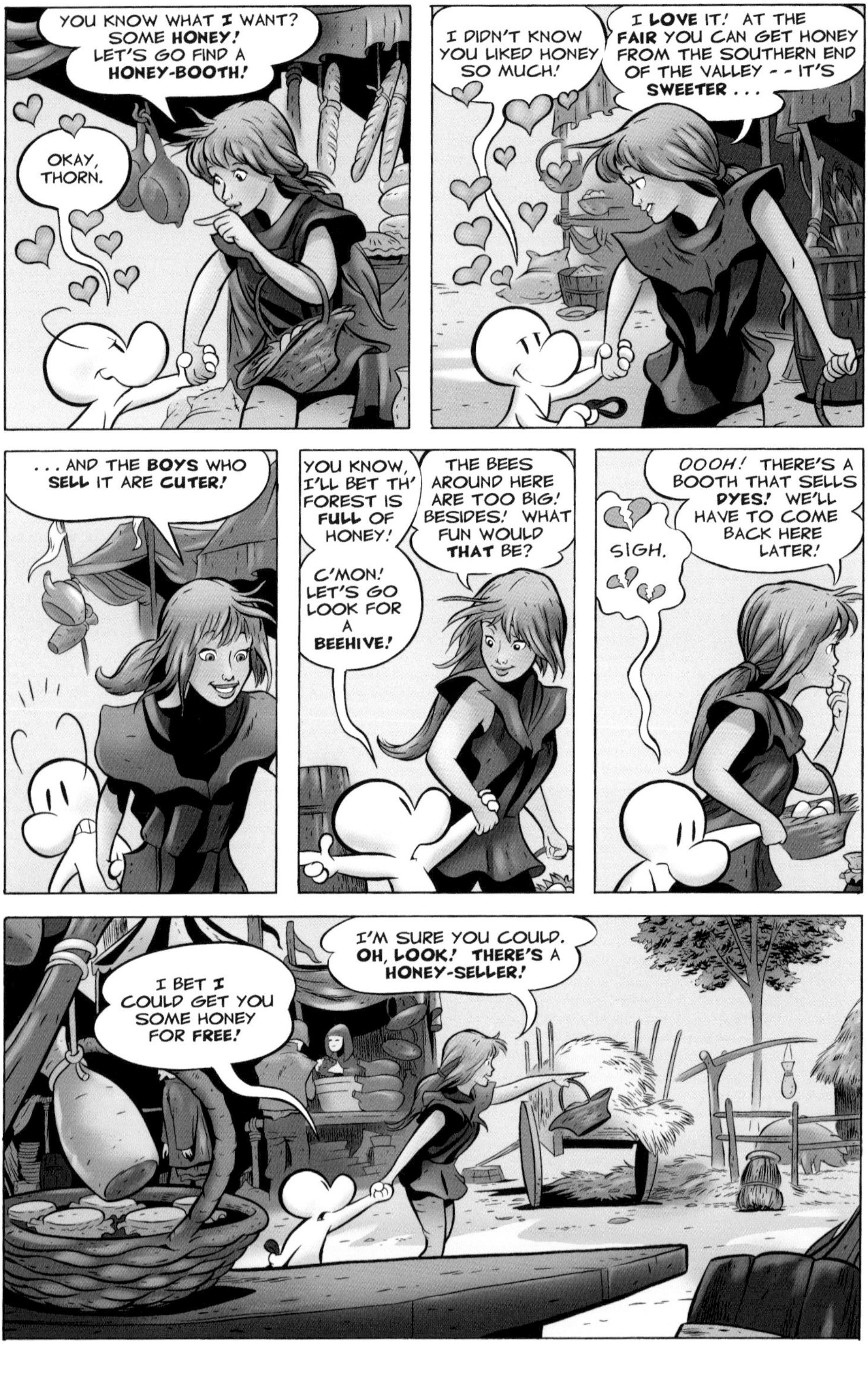
YOU KNOW WHAT I WANT? SOME HONEY! LET'S GO FIND A HONEY-BOOTH!
OKAY, THORN.
I DIDN'T KNOW YOU LIKED HONEY SO MUCH!
I LOVE IT! AT THE FAIR YOU CAN GET HONEY FROM THE SOUTHERN END OF THE VALLEY - - IT'S SWEETER . . .
. . . AND THE BOYS WHO SELL IT ARE CUTER!
YOU KNOW, I'LL BET TH' FOREST IS FULL OF HONEY!
C'MON! LET'S GO LOOK FOR A BEEHIVE!
THE BEES AROUND HERE ARE TOO BIG! BESIDES! WHAT FUN WOULD THAT BE?
SIGH.
OOOH! THERE'S A BOOTH THAT SELLS DYES! WE'LL HAVE TO COME BACK HERE LATER!
I BET I COULD GET YOU SOME HONEY FOR FREE!
I'M SURE YOU COULD. OH, LOOK! THERE'S A HONEY-SELLER!

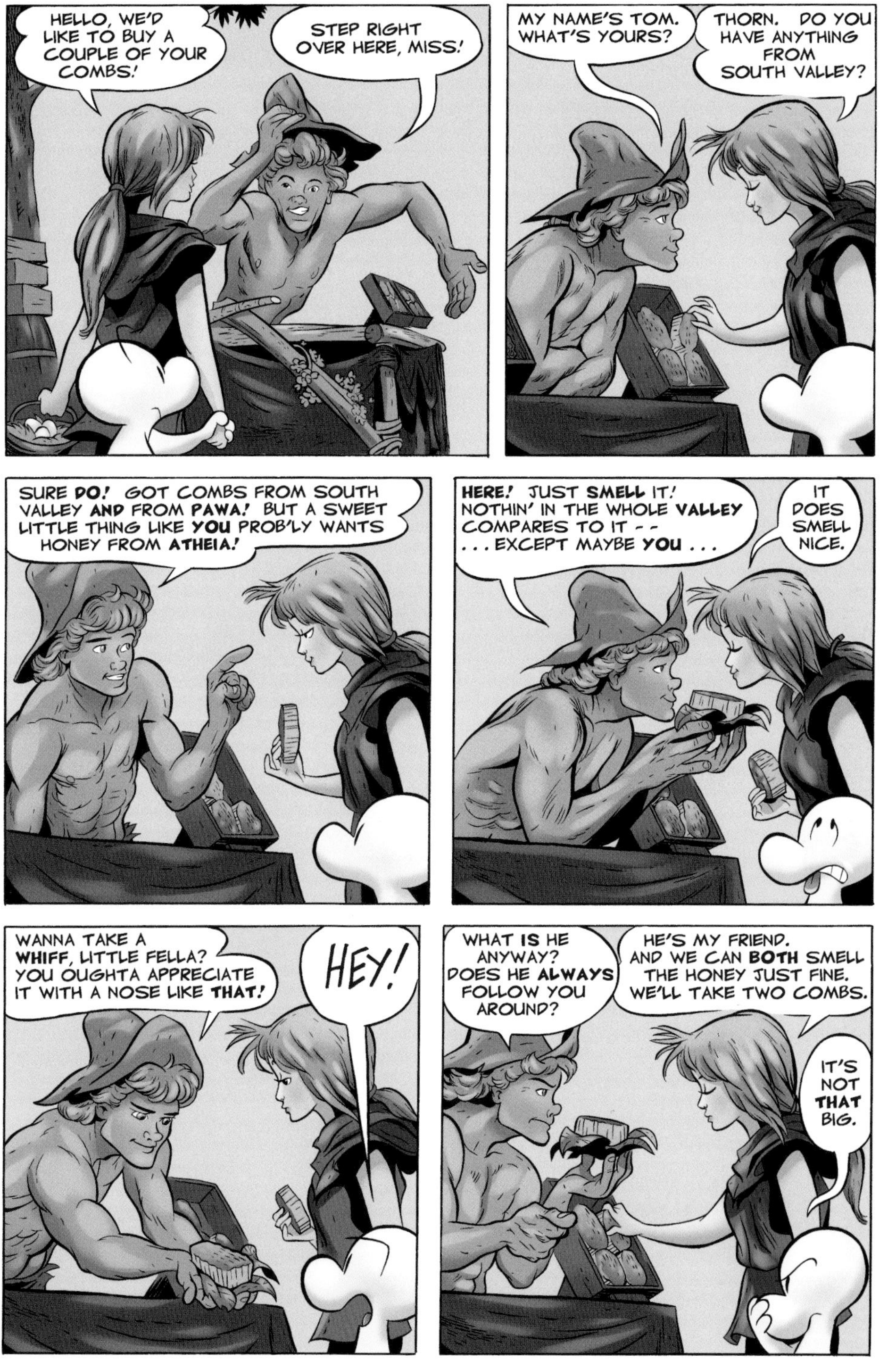
HELLO, WE'D LIKE TO BUY A COUPLE OF YOUR COMBS!
STEP RIGHT OVER HERE, MISS!
MY NAME'S TOM. WHAT'S YOURS?
THORN. DO YOU HAVE ANYTHING FROM SOUTH VALLEY?
SURE DO! GOT COMBS FROM SOUTH VALLEY AND FROM PAWA! BUT A SWEET LITTLE THING LIKE YOU PROB'LY WANTS HONEY FROM ATHEIA!
HERE! JUST SMELL IT! NOTHIN' IN THE WHOLE VALLEY COMPARES TO IT - - . . . EXCEPT MAYBE YOU . . .
IT DOES SMELL NICE.
WANNA TAKE A WHIFF, LITTLE FELLA? YOU OUGHTA APPRECIATE IT WITH A NOSE LIKE THAT!
HEY!
WHAT IS HE ANYWAY? DOES HE ALWAYS FOLLOW YOU AROUND?
HE'S MY FRIEND. AND WE CAN BOTH SMELL THE HONEY JUST FINE. WE'LL TAKE TWO COMBS.
IT'S NOT THAT BIG.

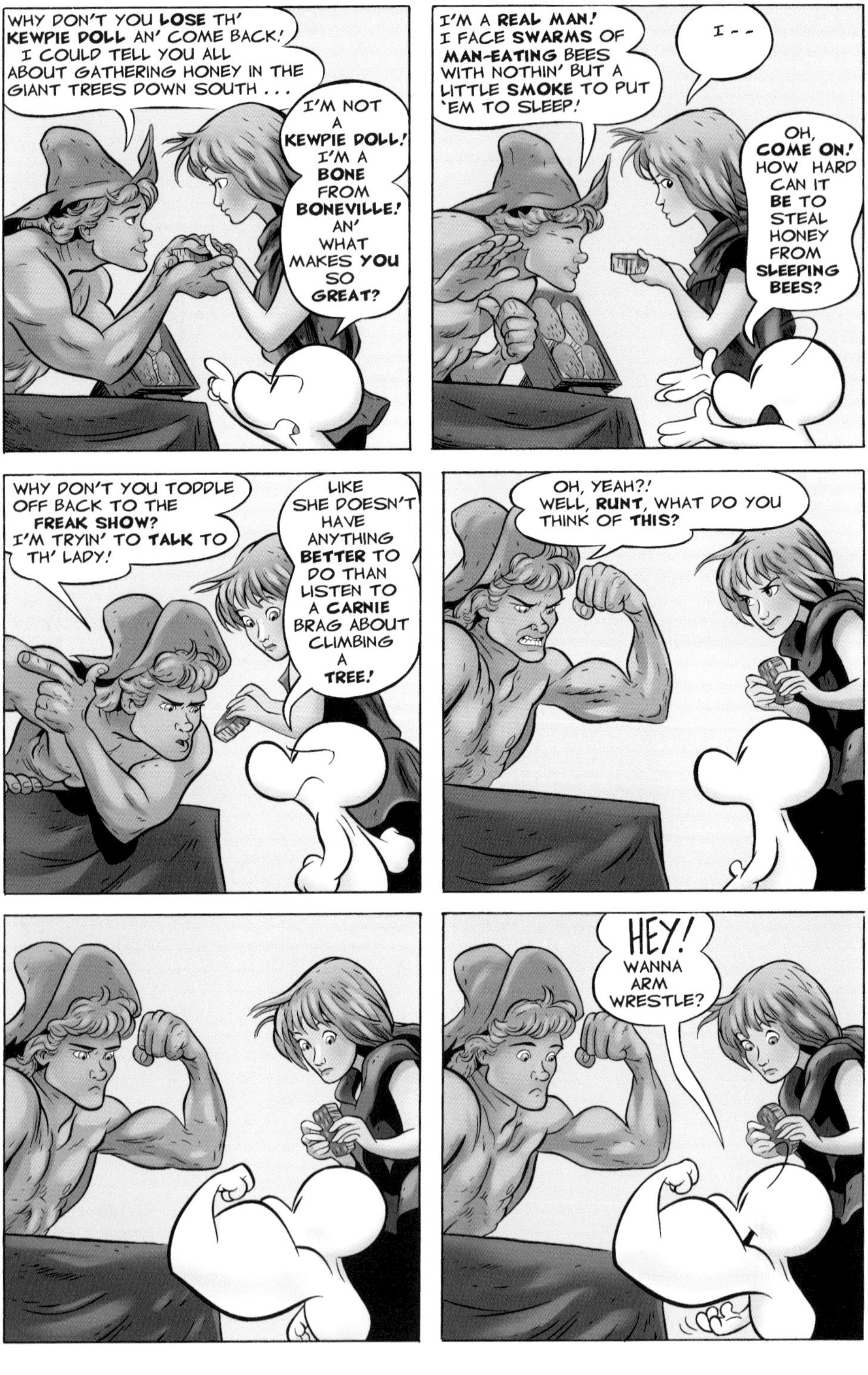
WHY DON'T YOU LOSE TH' KEWPIE DOLL AN' COME BACK! I COULD TELL YOU ALL ABOUT GATHERING HONEY IN THE GIANT TREES DOWN SOUTH . . .
I'M NOT A KEWPIE DOLL! I'M A BONE FROM BONEVILLE! AN' WHAT MAKES YOU SO GREAT?
I'M A REAL MAN! I FACE SWARMS OF MAN-EATING BEES WITH NOTHIN' BUT A LITTLE SMOKE TO PUT 'EM TO SLEEP!
I --
OH, COME ON! HOW HARD CAN IT BE TO STEAL HONEY FROM SLEEPING BEES?
WHY DON'T YOU TODDLE OFF BACK TO THE FREAK SHOW? I'M TRYIN' TO TALK TO TH' LADY!
LIKE SHE DOESN'T HAVE ANYTHING BETTER TO DO THAN LISTEN TO A CARNIE BRAG ABOUT CLIMBING A TREE!
OH, YEAH?! WELL, RUNT, WHAT DO YOU THINK OF THIS?
HEY! WANNA ARM WRESTLE?

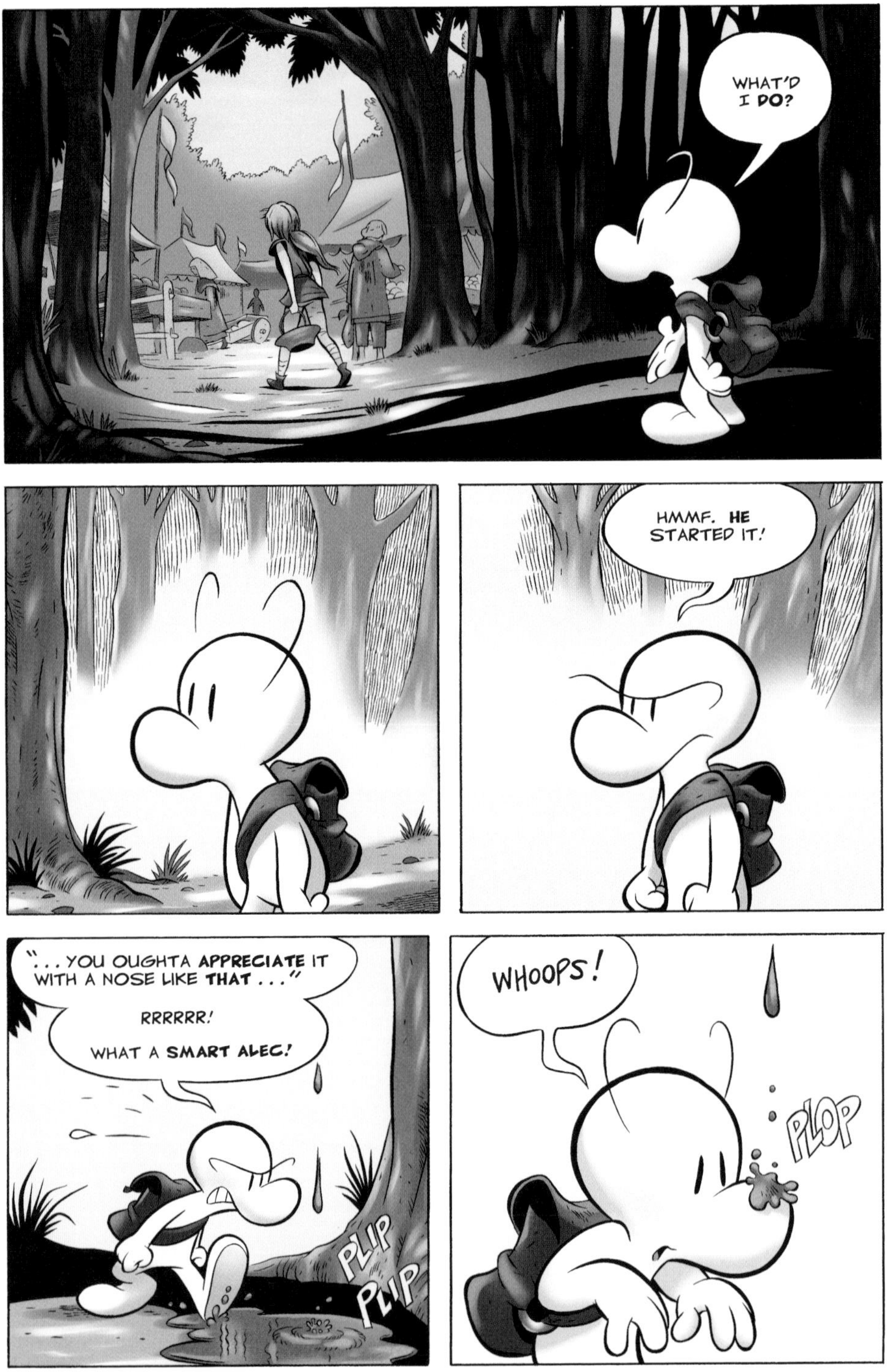
WHAT'D I DO?
HMMF. HE STARTED IT!
"...YOU OUGHTA APPRECIATE IT WITH A NOSE LIKE THAT..."
RRRRRR!
WHAT A SMART ALEC!
PLIP
PLIP
WHOOPS!
PLOP

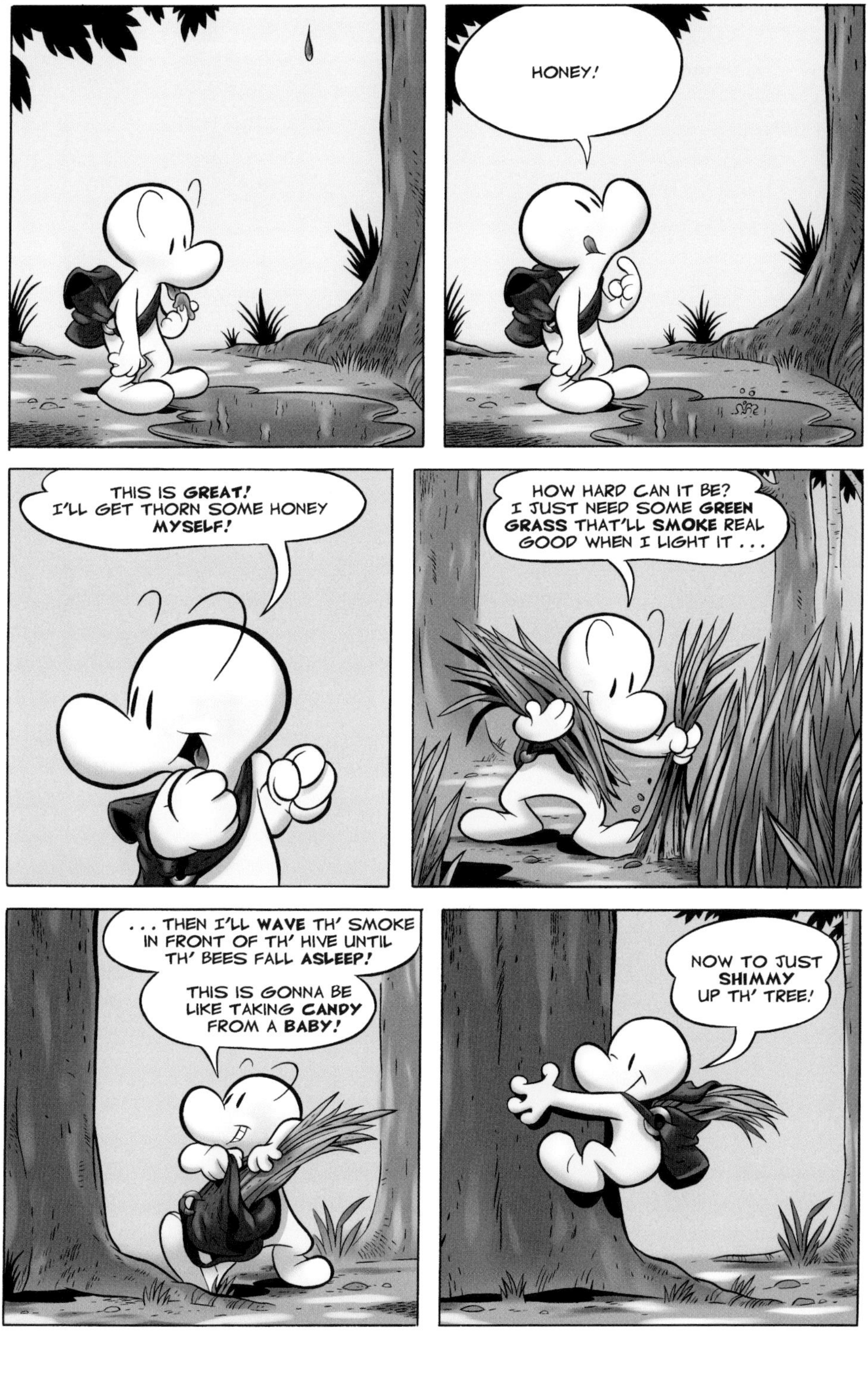
HONEY!
THIS IS GREAT! I'LL GET THORN SOME HONEY MYSELF!
HOW HARD CAN IT BE? I JUST NEED SOME GREEN GRASS THAT'LL SMOKE REAL GOOD WHEN I LIGHT IT . . .
. . . THEN I'LL WAVE TH' SMOKE IN FRONT OF TH' HIVE UNTIL TH' BEES FALL ASLEEP!
THIS IS GONNA BE LIKE TAKING CANDY FROM A BABY!
NOW TO JUST SHIMMY UP TH' TREE!

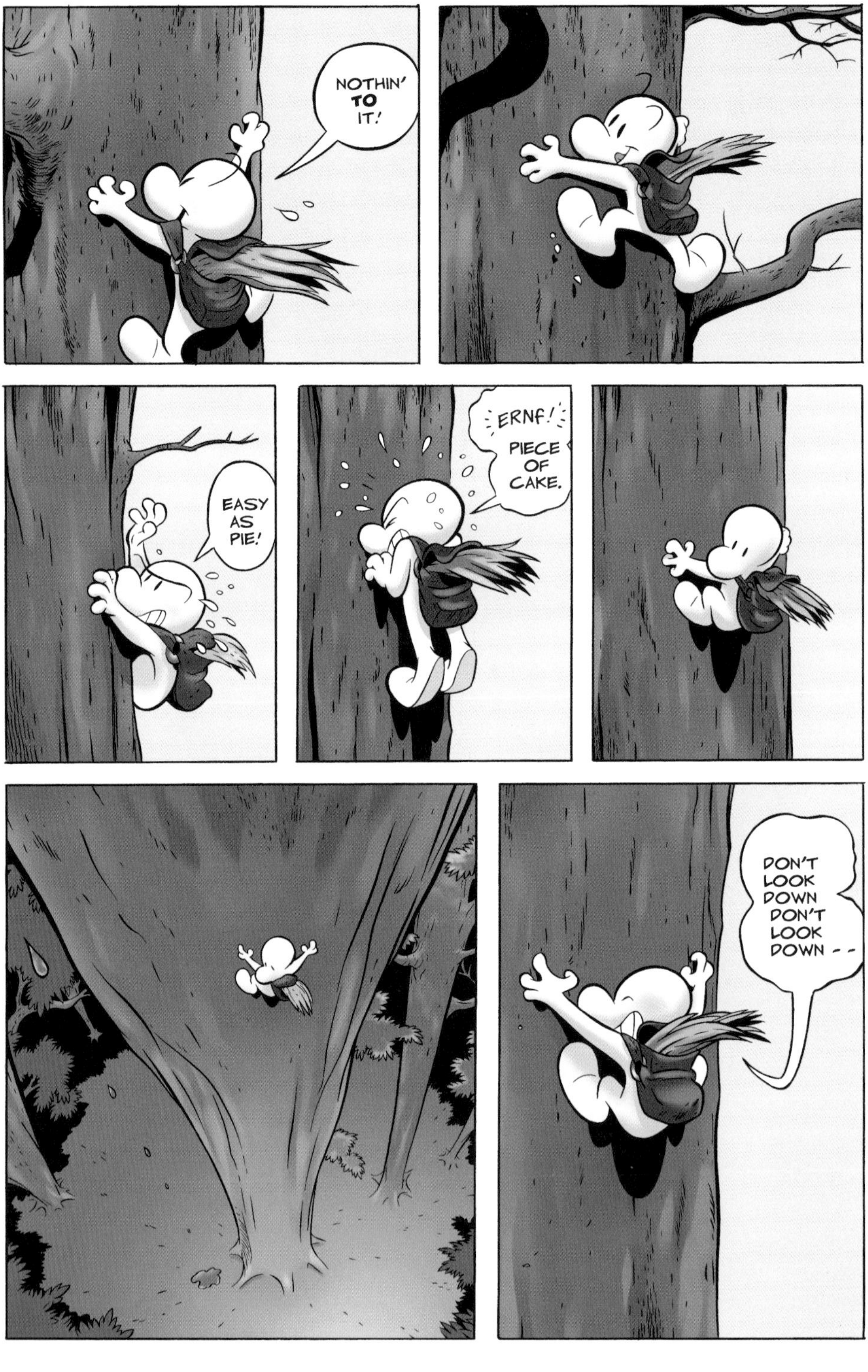
NOTHIN' TO IT!
EASY AS PIE!
ERNF! PIECE OF CAKE.
DON'T LOOK DOWN DON'T LOOK DOWN - -

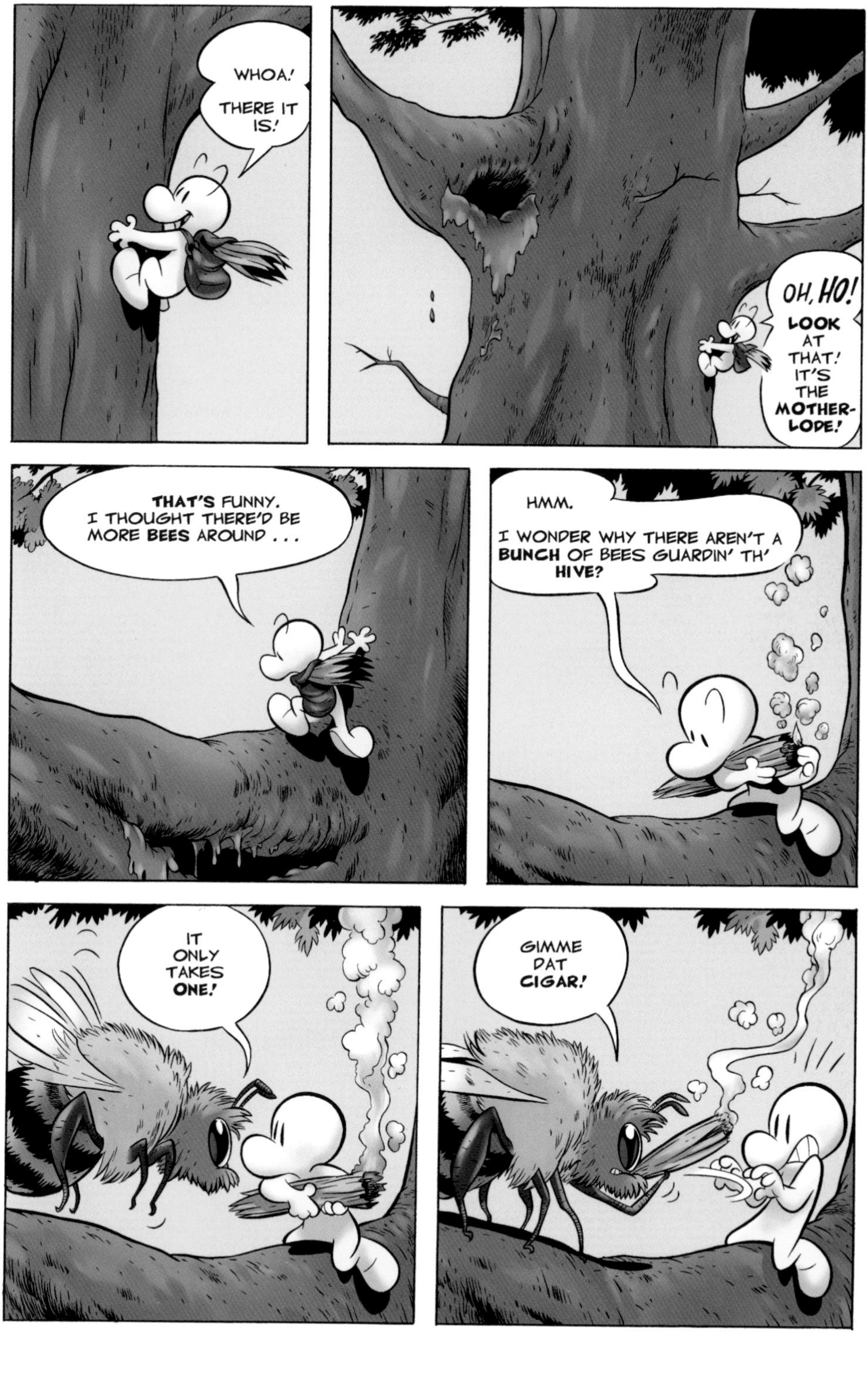
WHOA! THERE IT IS!
OH, HO! LOOK AT THAT! IT'S THE MOTHER-LODE!
THAT'S FUNNY. I THOUGHT THERE'D BE MORE BEES AROUND . . .
HMM.
I WONDER WHY THERE AREN'T A BUNCH OF BEES GUARDIN' TH' HIVE?
IT ONLY TAKES ONE!
GIMME DAT CIGAR!

LET'S GO, LET'S GO! THIS FOOD'S BEEN UP HERE FOR **THREE SECONDS** ALREADY! YOU WANT IT TO GET **COLD?**

COMIN', PHONEY! 'SCUSE ME A MOMENT, FELLAS.

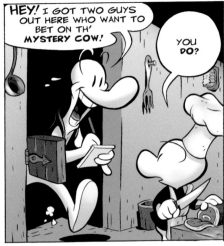

HEY! I GOT TWO GUYS OUT HERE WHO WANT TO BET ON TH' **MYSTERY COW!**

YOU DO?

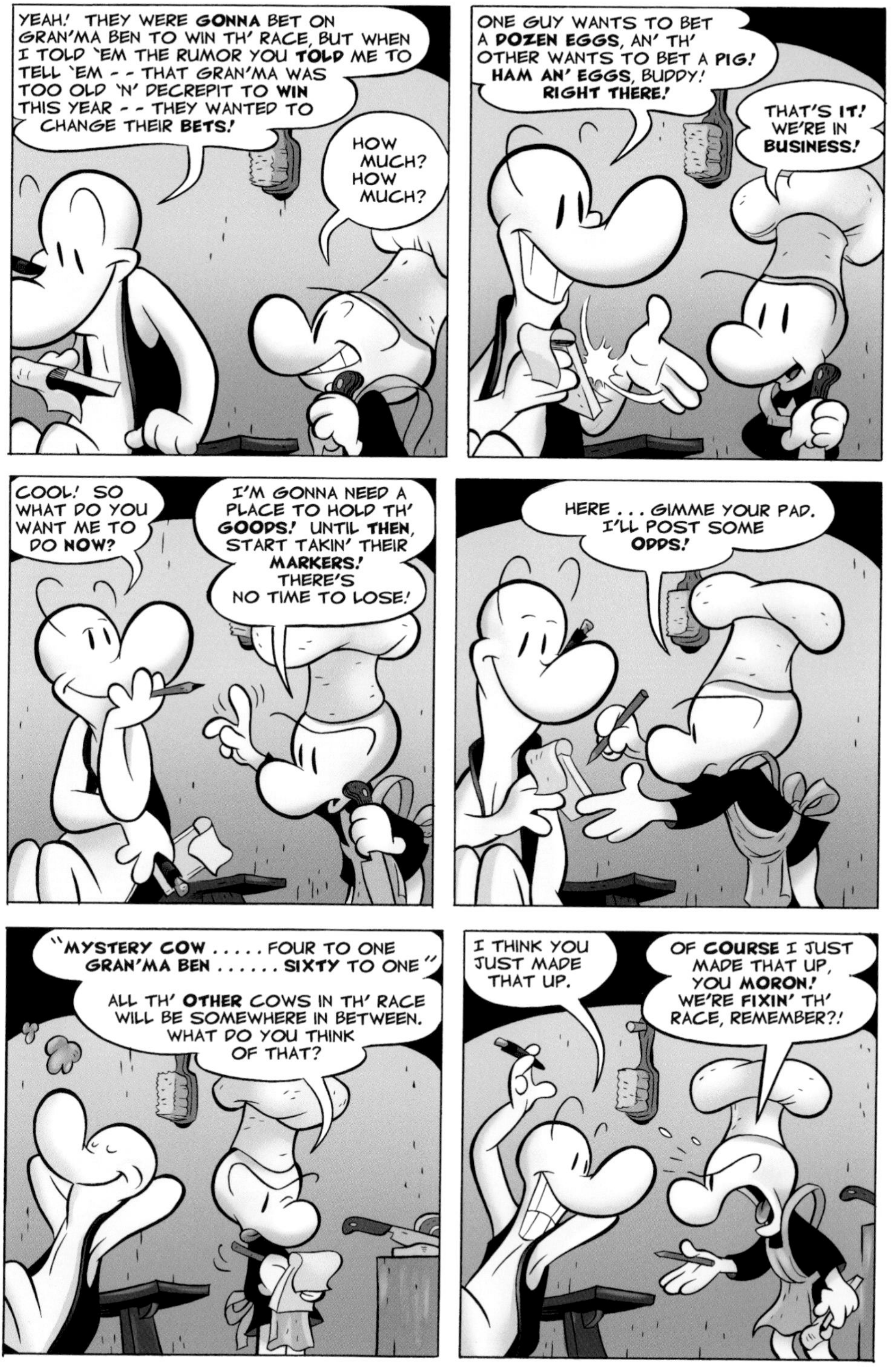
YEAH! THEY WERE GONNA BET ON GRAN'MA BEN TO WIN TH' RACE, BUT WHEN I TOLD 'EM THE RUMOR YOU TOLD ME TO TELL 'EM - - THAT GRAN'MA WAS TOO OLD 'N' DECREPIT TO WIN THIS YEAR - - THEY WANTED TO CHANGE THEIR BETS!
HOW MUCH? HOW MUCH?
ONE GUY WANTS TO BET A DOZEN EGGS, AN' TH' OTHER WANTS TO BET A PIG! HAM AN' EGGS, BUDDY! RIGHT THERE!
THAT'S IT! WE'RE IN BUSINESS!
COOL! SO WHAT DO YOU WANT ME TO DO NOW?
I'M GONNA NEED A PLACE TO HOLD TH' GOODS! UNTIL THEN, START TAKIN' THEIR MARKERS! THERE'S NO TIME TO LOSE!
HERE . . . GIMME YOUR PAD. I'LL POST SOME ODDS!
"MYSTERY COW . . . . . FOUR TO ONE GRAN'MA BEN . . . . . . SIXTY TO ONE"
ALL TH' OTHER COWS IN TH' RACE WILL BE SOMEWHERE IN BETWEEN. WHAT DO YOU THINK OF THAT?
I THINK YOU JUST MADE THAT UP.
OF COURSE I JUST MADE THAT UP, YOU MORON! WE'RE FIXIN' TH' RACE, REMEMBER?!

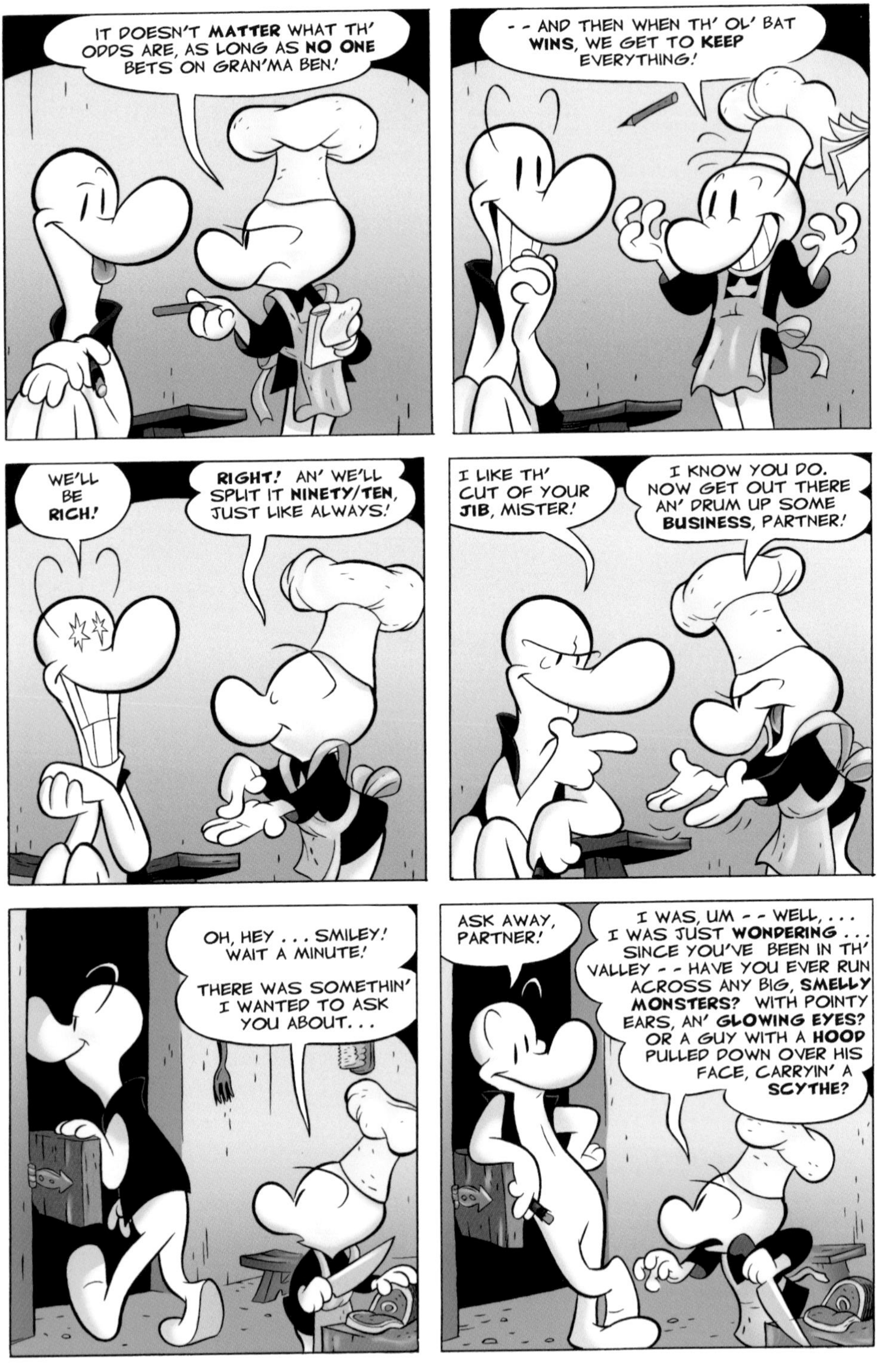
IT DOESN'T MATTER WHAT TH' ODDS ARE, AS LONG AS NO ONE BETS ON GRAN'MA BEN!
- - AND THEN WHEN TH' OL' BAT WINS, WE GET TO KEEP EVERYTHING!
WE'LL BE RICH!
RIGHT! AN' WE'LL SPLIT IT NINETY/TEN, JUST LIKE ALWAYS!
I LIKE TH' CUT OF YOUR JIB, MISTER!
I KNOW YOU DO. NOW GET OUT THERE AN' DRUM UP SOME BUSINESS, PARTNER!
OH, HEY . . . SMILEY! WAIT A MINUTE!
THERE WAS SOMETHIN' I WANTED TO ASK YOU ABOUT. . .
ASK AWAY, PARTNER!
I WAS, UM - - WELL, . . . I WAS JUST WONDERING . . . SINCE YOU'VE BEEN IN TH' VALLEY - - HAVE YOU EVER RUN ACROSS ANY BIG, SMELLY MONSTERS? WITH POINTY EARS, AN' GLOWING EYES? OR A GUY WITH A HOOD PULLED DOWN OVER HIS FACE, CARRYIN' A SCYTHE?

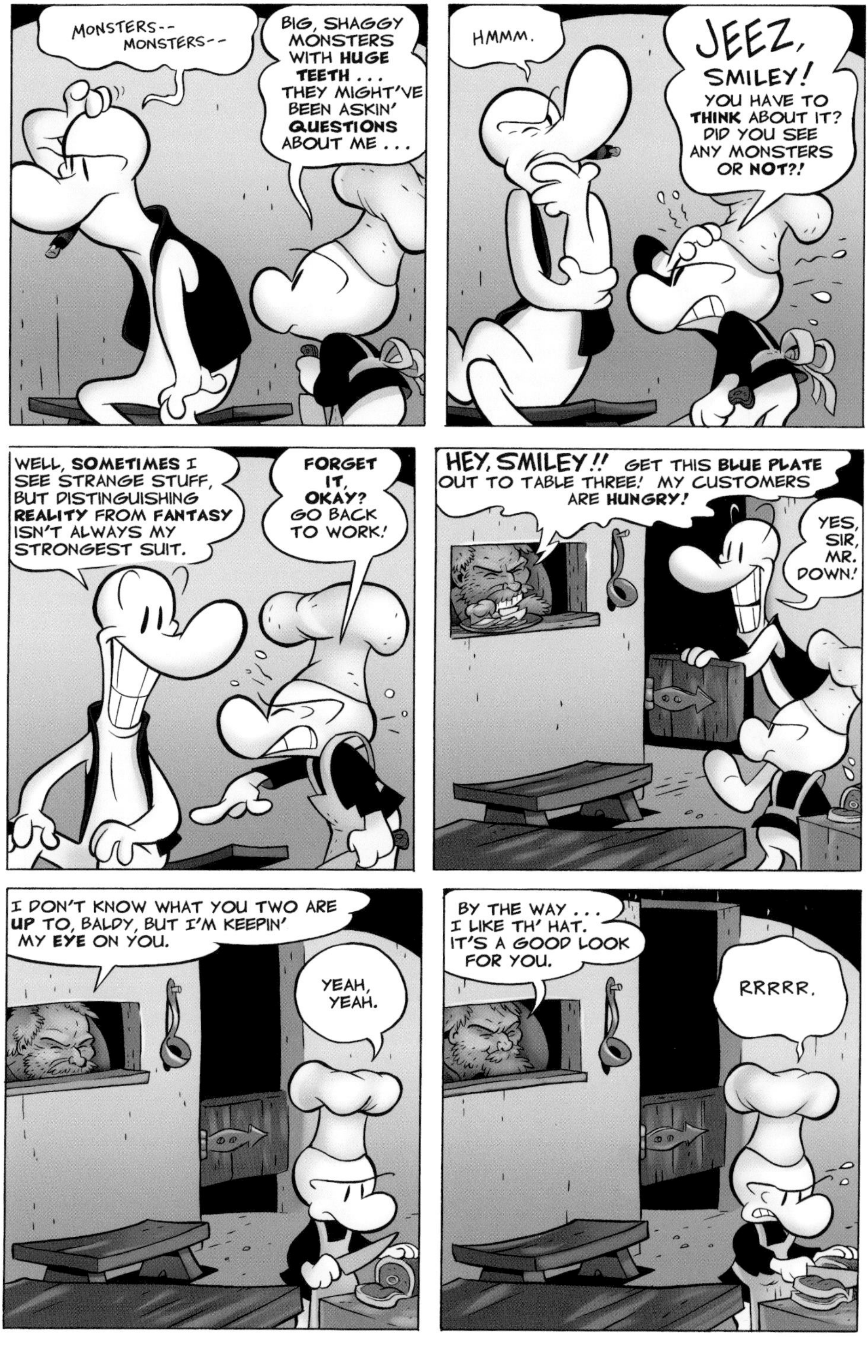
MONSTERS-- MONSTERS--
BIG, SHAGGY MONSTERS WITH HUGE TEETH . . . THEY MIGHT'VE BEEN ASKIN' QUESTIONS ABOUT ME . . .
HMMM.
JEEZ, SMILEY! YOU HAVE TO THINK ABOUT IT? DID YOU SEE ANY MONSTERS OR NOT?!
WELL, SOMETIMES I SEE STRANGE STUFF, BUT DISTINGUISHING REALITY FROM FANTASY ISN'T ALWAYS MY STRONGEST SUIT.
FORGET IT, OKAY? GO BACK TO WORK!
HEY, SMILEY!! GET THIS BLUE PLATE OUT TO TABLE THREE! MY CUSTOMERS ARE HUNGRY!
YES, SIR, MR. DOWN!
I DON'T KNOW WHAT YOU TWO ARE UP TO, BALDY, BUT I'M KEEPIN' MY EYE ON YOU.
YEAH, YEAH.
BY THE WAY . . . I LIKE TH' HAT. IT'S A GOOD LOOK FOR YOU.
RRRRR.

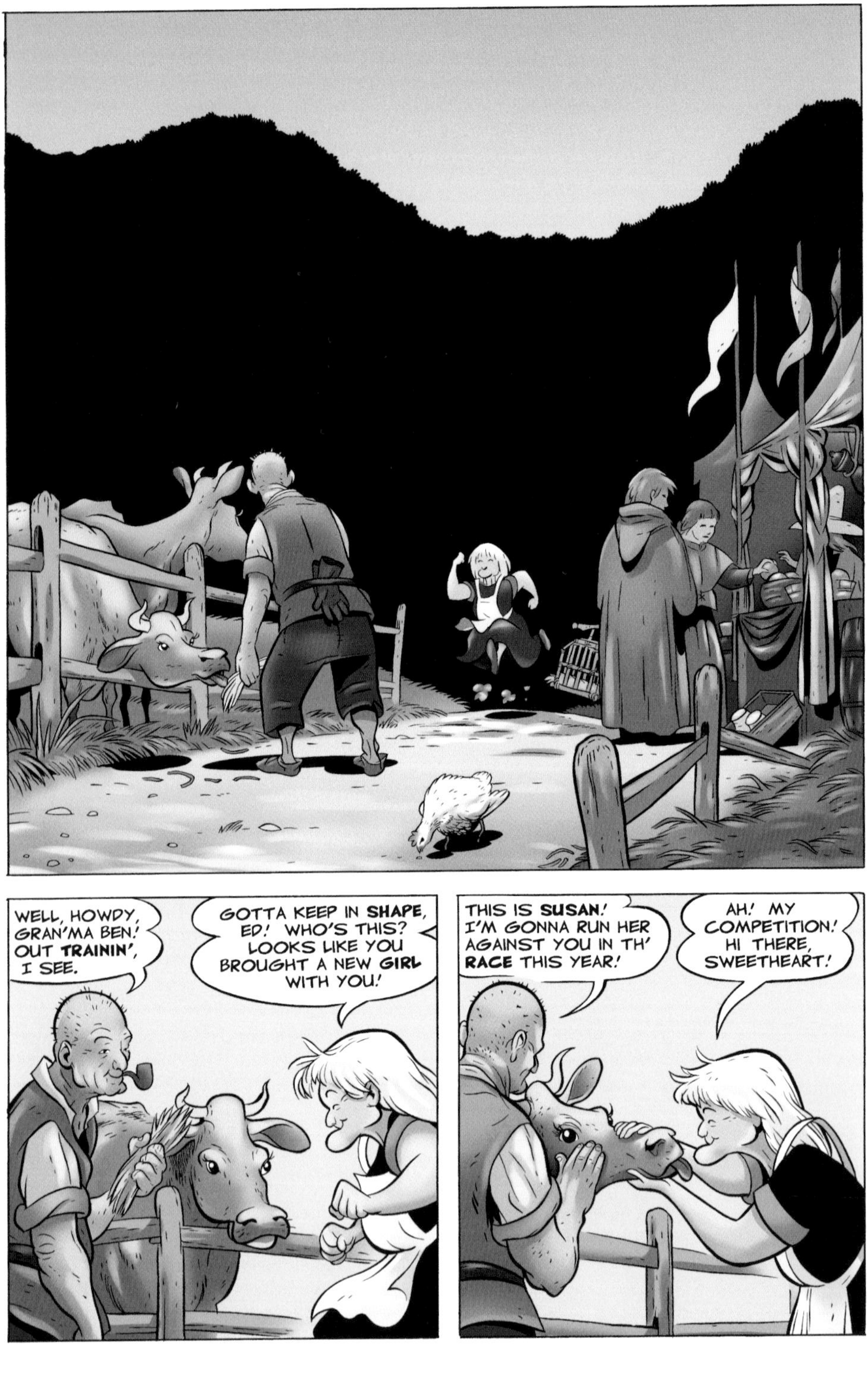
WELL, HOWDY, GRAN'MA BEN! OUT TRAININ', I SEE.
GOTTA KEEP IN SHAPE, ED! WHO'S THIS? LOOKS LIKE YOU BROUGHT A NEW GIRL WITH YOU!
THIS IS SUSAN! I'M GONNA RUN HER AGAINST YOU IN TH' RACE THIS YEAR!
AH! MY COMPETITION! HI THERE, SWEETHEART!

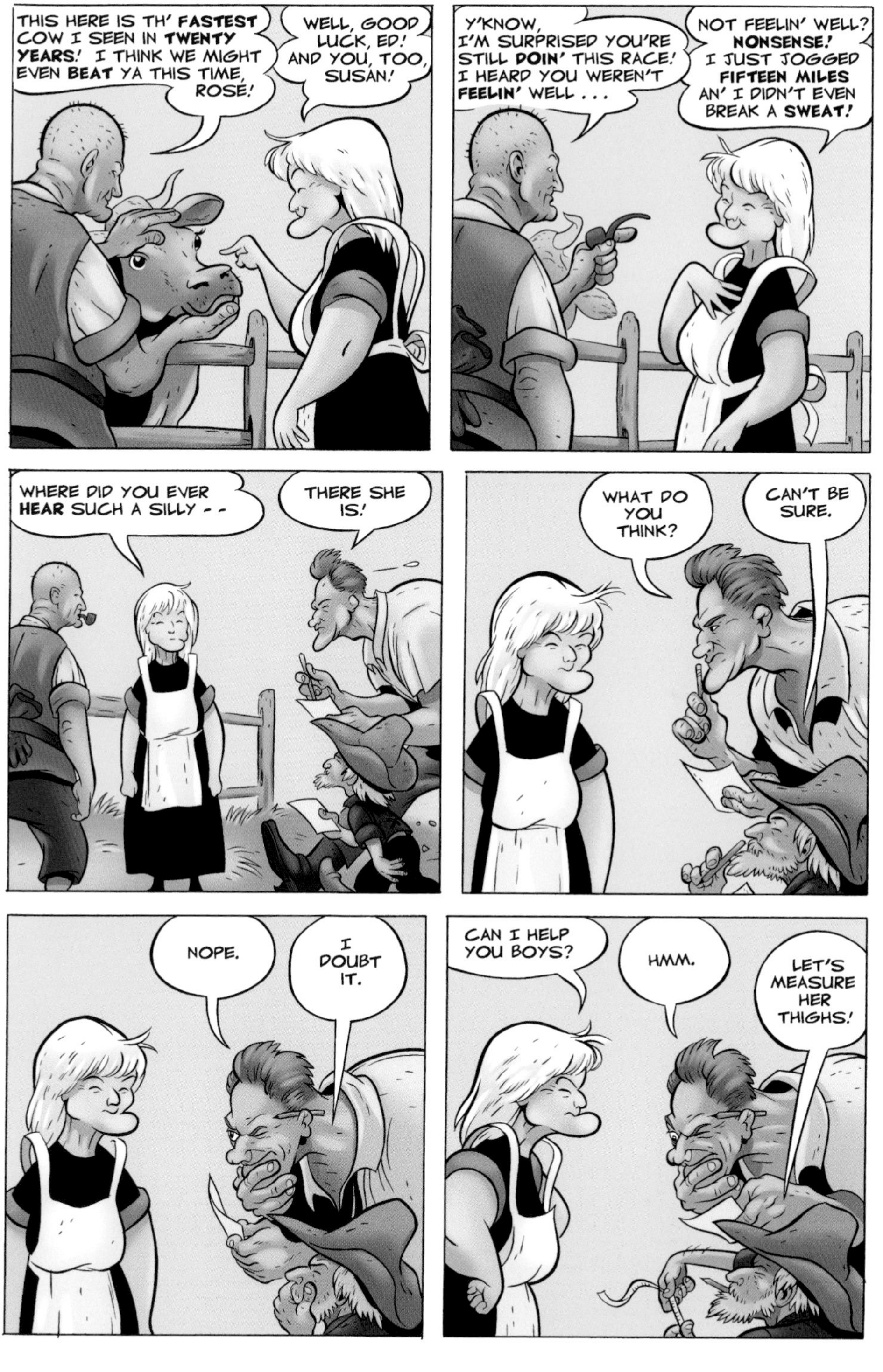
THIS HERE IS TH' FASTEST COW I SEEN IN TWENTY YEARS! I THINK WE MIGHT EVEN BEAT YA THIS TIME, ROSE!
WELL, GOOD LUCK, ED! AND YOU, TOO, SUSAN!
Y'KNOW, I'M SURPRISED YOU'RE STILL DOIN' THIS RACE! I HEARD YOU WEREN'T FEELIN' WELL . . .
NOT FEELIN' WELL? NONSENSE! I JUST JOGGED FIFTEEN MILES AN' I DIDN'T EVEN BREAK A SWEAT!
WHERE DID YOU EVER HEAR SUCH A SILLY - -
THERE SHE IS!
WHAT DO YOU THINK?
CAN'T BE SURE.
NOPE.
I DOUBT IT.
CAN I HELP YOU BOYS?
HMM.
LET'S MEASURE HER THIGHS!

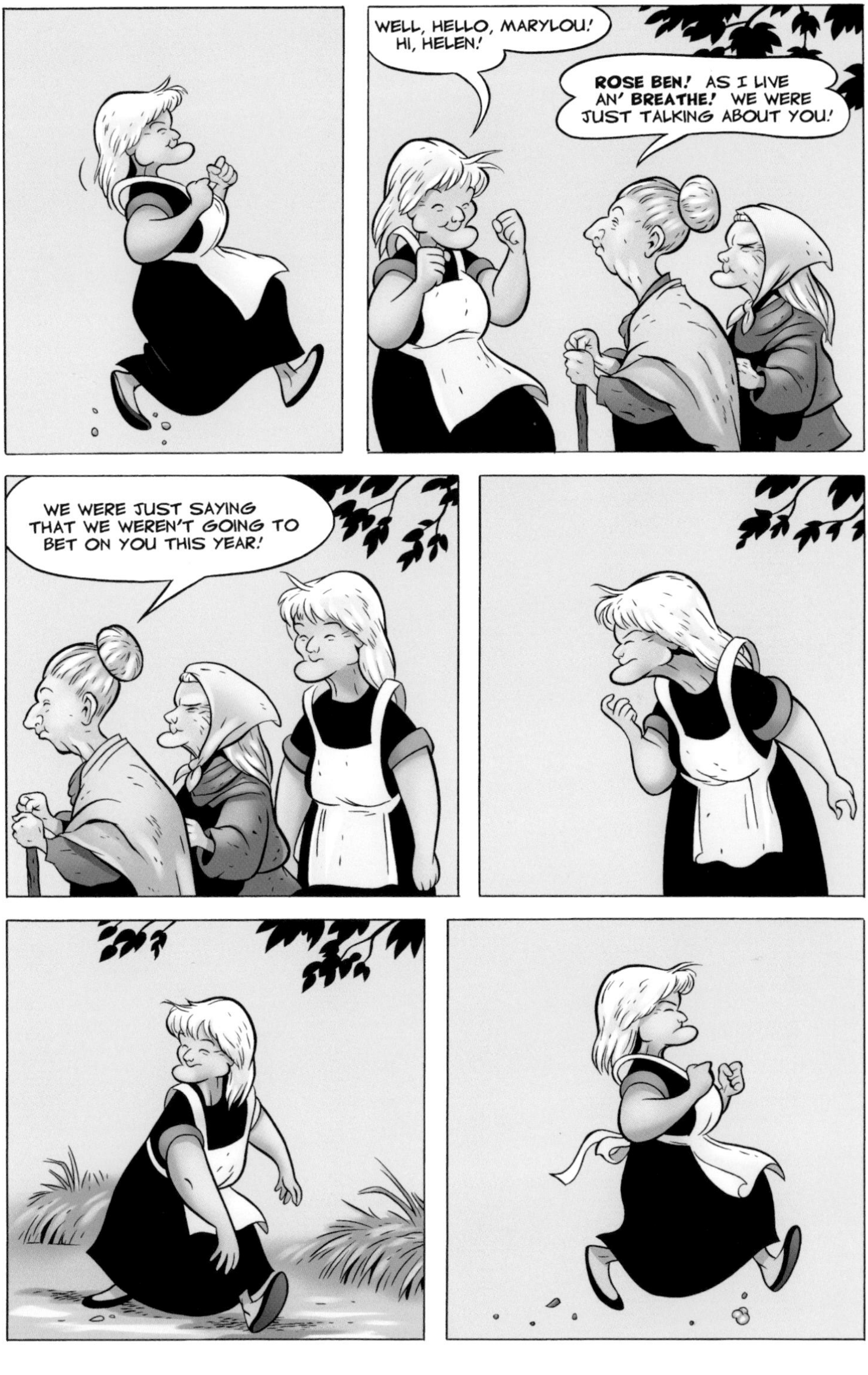
WELL, HELLO, MARYLOU! HI, HELEN!
ROSE BEN! AS I LIVE AN' BREATHE! WE WERE JUST TALKING ABOUT YOU!
WE WERE JUST SAYING THAT WE WEREN'T GOING TO BET ON YOU THIS YEAR!

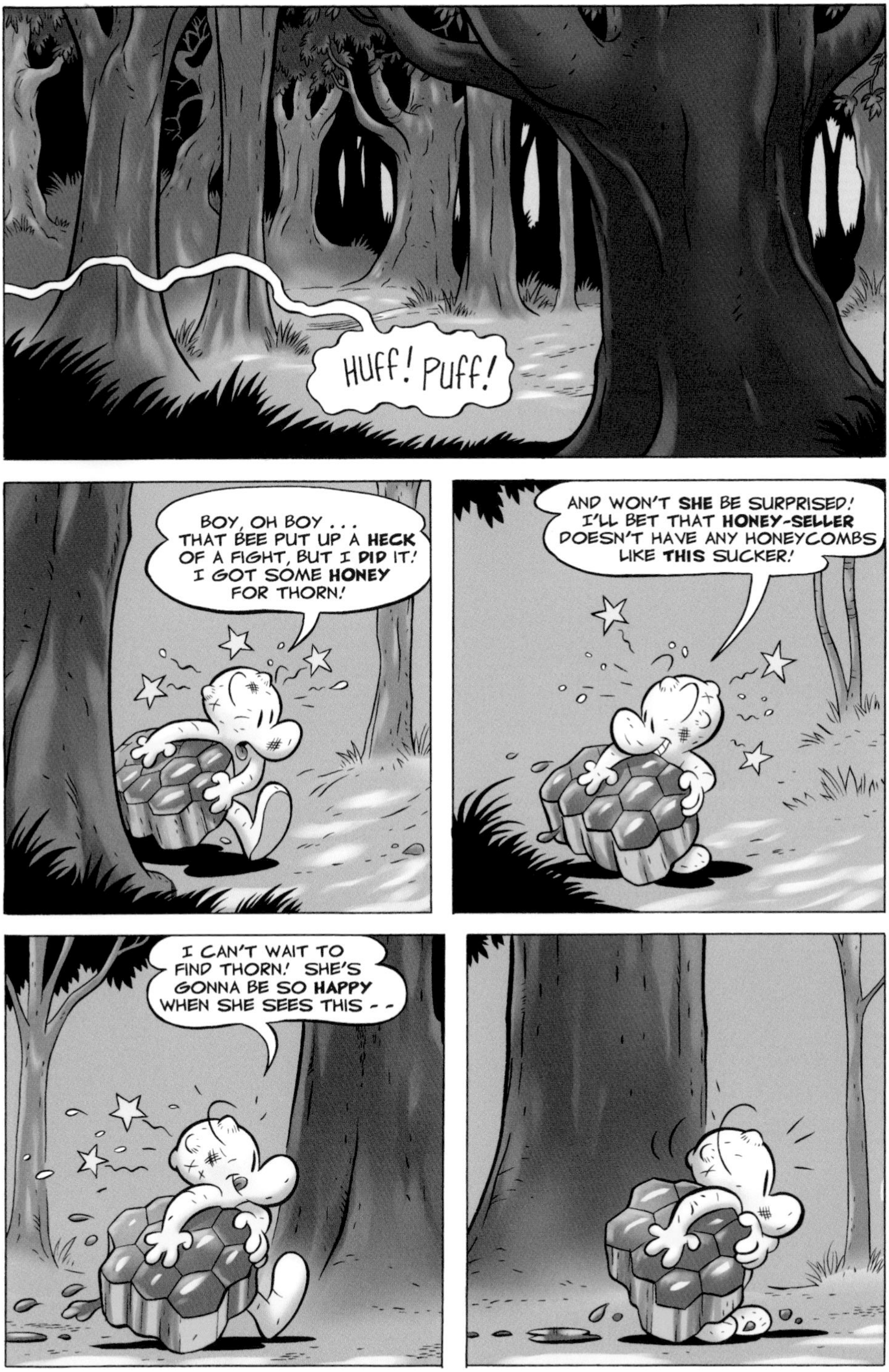
HUFF! PUFF!
BOY, OH BOY . . . THAT BEE PUT UP A HECK OF A FIGHT, BUT I DID IT! I GOT SOME HONEY FOR THORN!
AND WON'T SHE BE SURPRISED! I'LL BET THAT HONEY-SELLER DOESN'T HAVE ANY HONEYCOMBS LIKE THIS SUCKER!
I CAN'T WAIT TO FIND THORN! SHE'S GONNA BE SO HAPPY WHEN SHE SEES THIS - -

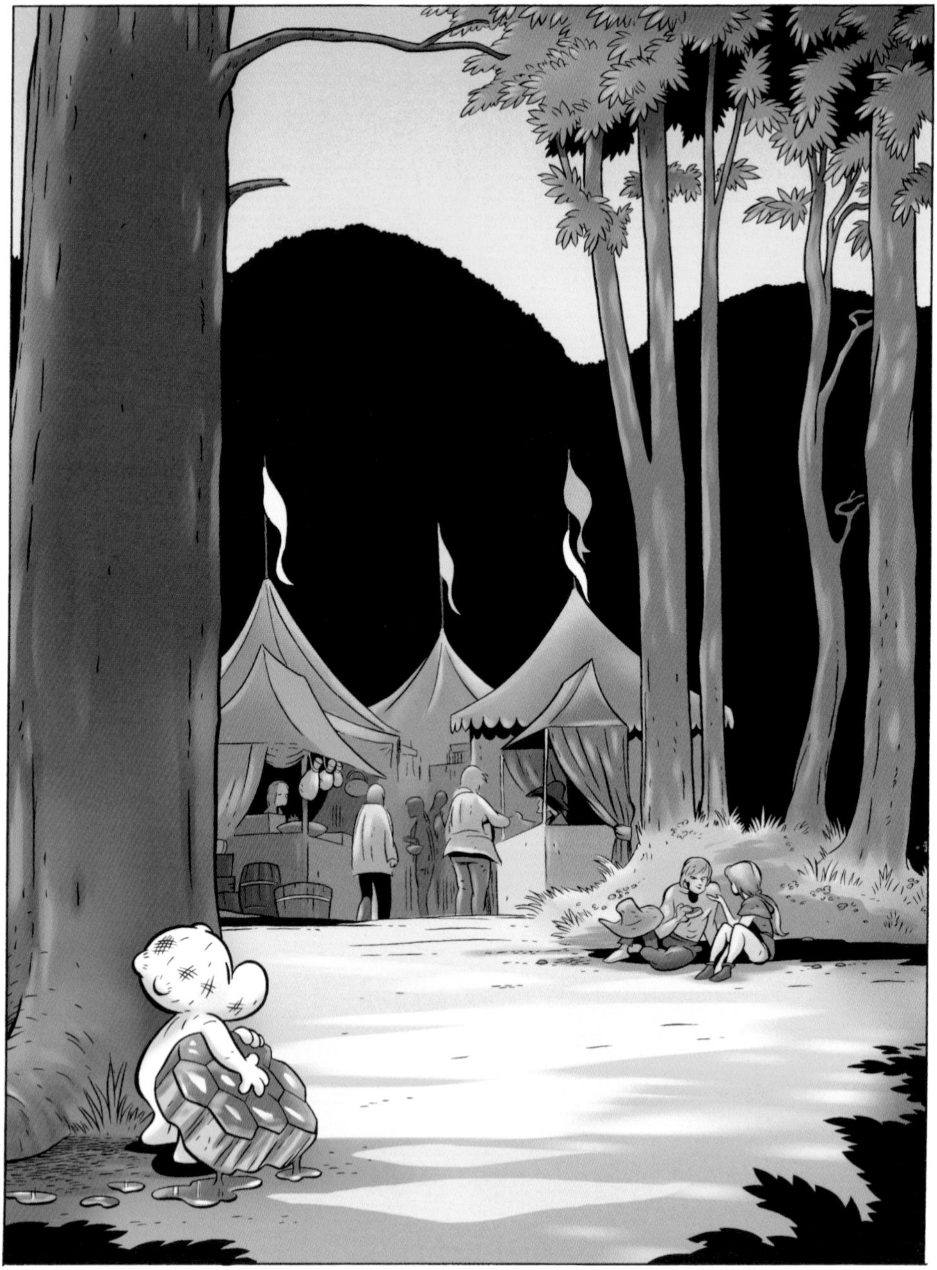

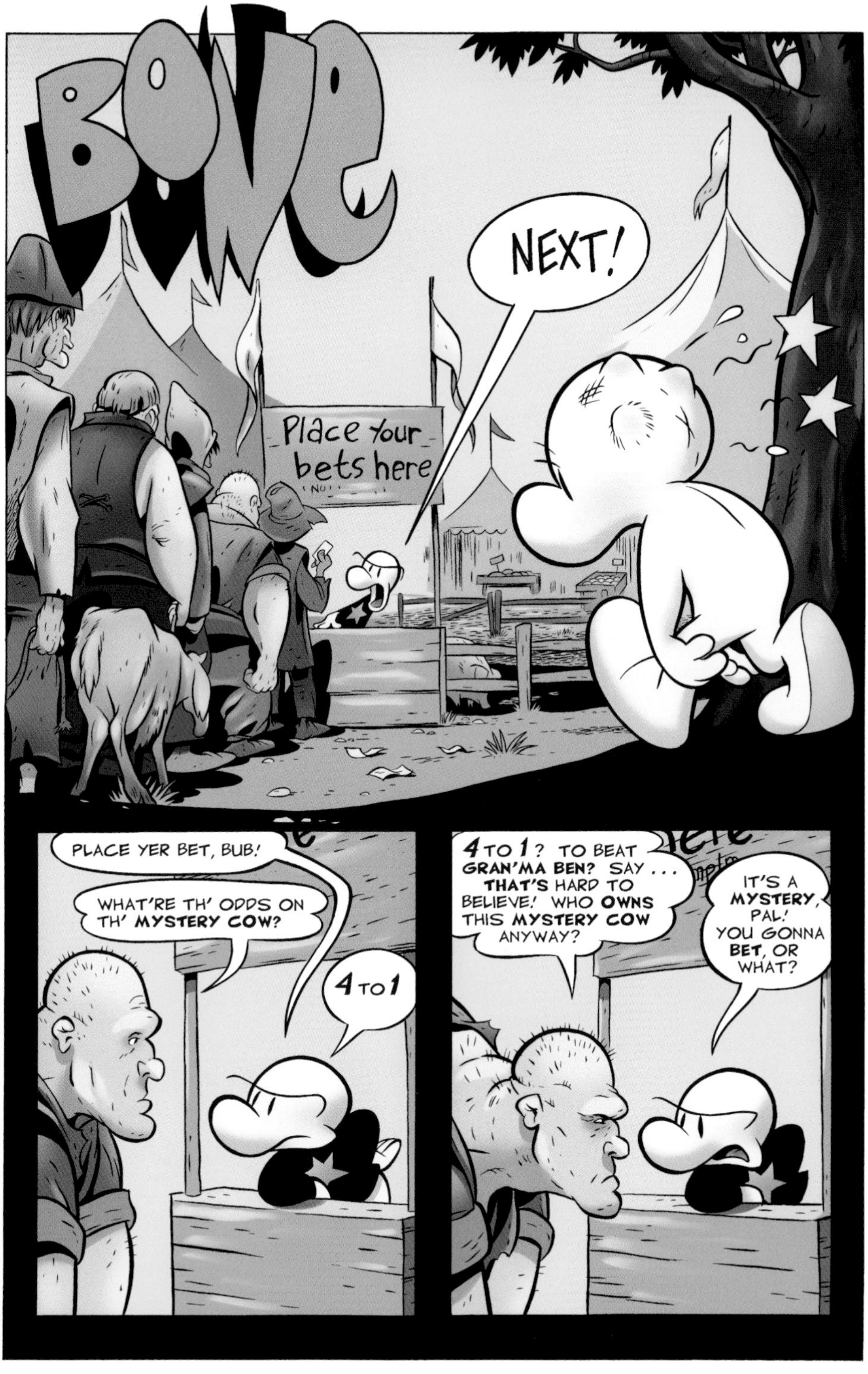
BONE
NEXT!
Place your bets here
PLACE YER BET, BUB!
WHAT'RE TH' ODDS ON TH' MYSTERY COW?
4 TO 1
4 TO 1? TO BEAT GRAN'MA BEN? SAY... THAT'S HARD TO BELIEVE! WHO OWNS THIS MYSTERY COW ANYWAY?
IT'S A MYSTERY, PAL! YOU GONNA BET, OR WHAT?

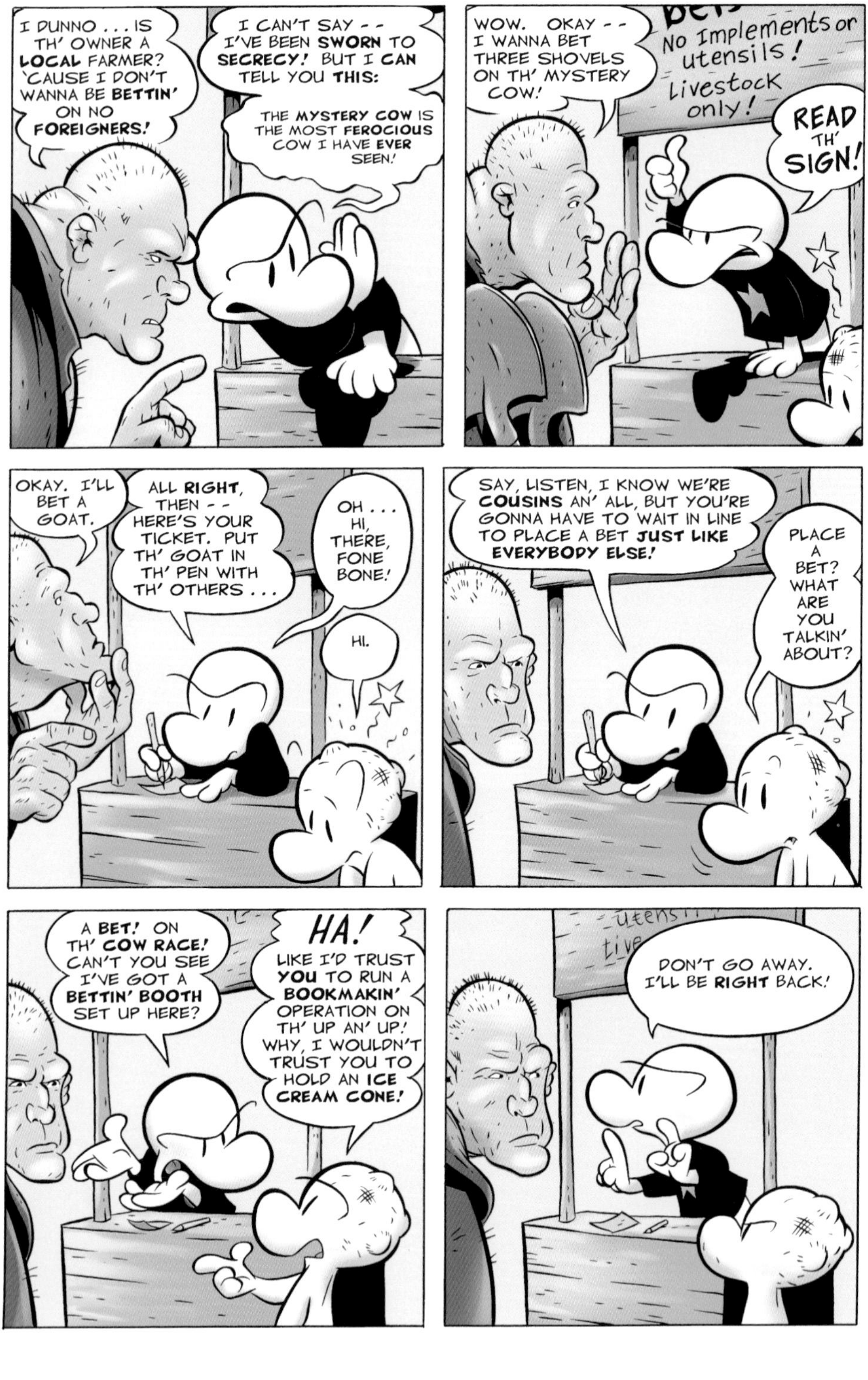
I DUNNO . . . IS TH' OWNER A LOCAL FARMER? 'CAUSE I DON'T WANNA BE BETTIN' ON NO FOREIGNERS!
I CAN'T SAY - - I'VE BEEN SWORN TO SECRECY! BUT I CAN TELL YOU THIS:
THE MYSTERY COW IS THE MOST FEROCIOUS COW I HAVE EVER SEEN!
WOW. OKAY - - I WANNA BET THREE SHOVELS ON TH' MYSTERY COW!
No Implements or utensils! Livestock only!
READ TH' SIGN!
OKAY. I'LL BET A GOAT.
ALL RIGHT, THEN - - HERE'S YOUR TICKET. PUT TH' GOAT IN TH' PEN WITH TH' OTHERS . . .
OH . . . HI, THERE, FONE BONE!
HI.
SAY, LISTEN, I KNOW WE'RE COUSINS AN' ALL, BUT YOU'RE GONNA HAVE TO WAIT IN LINE TO PLACE A BET JUST LIKE EVERYBODY ELSE!
PLACE A BET? WHAT ARE YOU TALKIN' ABOUT?
A BET! ON TH' COW RACE! CAN'T YOU SEE I'VE GOT A BETTIN' BOOTH SET UP HERE?
HA!
LIKE I'D TRUST YOU TO RUN A BOOKMAKIN' OPERATION ON TH' UP AN' UP! WHY, I WOULDN'T TRUST YOU TO HOLD AN ICE CREAM CONE!
DON'T GO AWAY. I'LL BE RIGHT BACK!

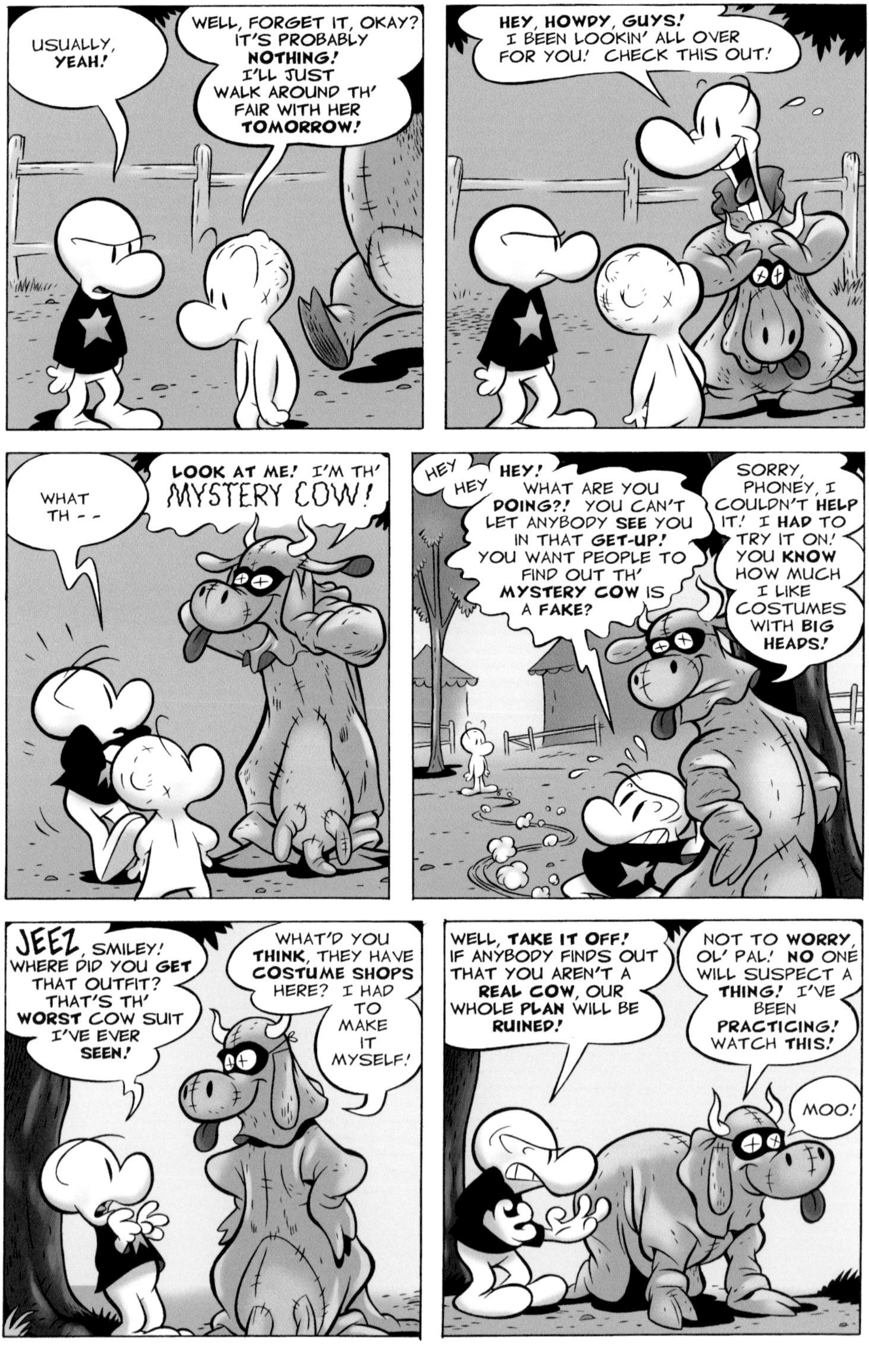
USUALLY, YEAH!
WELL, FORGET IT, OKAY? IT'S PROBABLY NOTHING! I'LL JUST WALK AROUND TH' FAIR WITH HER TOMORROW!
HEY, HOWDY, GUYS! I BEEN LOOKIN' ALL OVER FOR YOU! CHECK THIS OUT!
WHAT TH - -
LOOK AT ME! I'M TH' MYSTERY COW!
HEY
HEY
HEY! WHAT ARE YOU DOING?! YOU CAN'T LET ANYBODY SEE YOU IN THAT GET-UP! YOU WANT PEOPLE TO FIND OUT TH' MYSTERY COW IS A FAKE?
SORRY, PHONEY, I COULDN'T HELP IT! I HAD TO TRY IT ON! YOU KNOW HOW MUCH I LIKE COSTUMES WITH BIG HEADS!
JEEZ, SMILEY! WHERE DID YOU GET THAT OUTFIT? THAT'S TH' WORST COW SUIT I'VE EVER SEEN!
WHAT'D YOU THINK, THEY HAVE COSTUME SHOPS HERE? I HAD TO MAKE IT MYSELF!
WELL, TAKE IT OFF! IF ANYBODY FINDS OUT THAT YOU AREN'T A REAL COW, OUR WHOLE PLAN WILL BE RUINED!
NOT TO WORRY, OL' PAL! NO ONE WILL SUSPECT A THING! I'VE BEEN PRACTICING! WATCH THIS!
MOO!

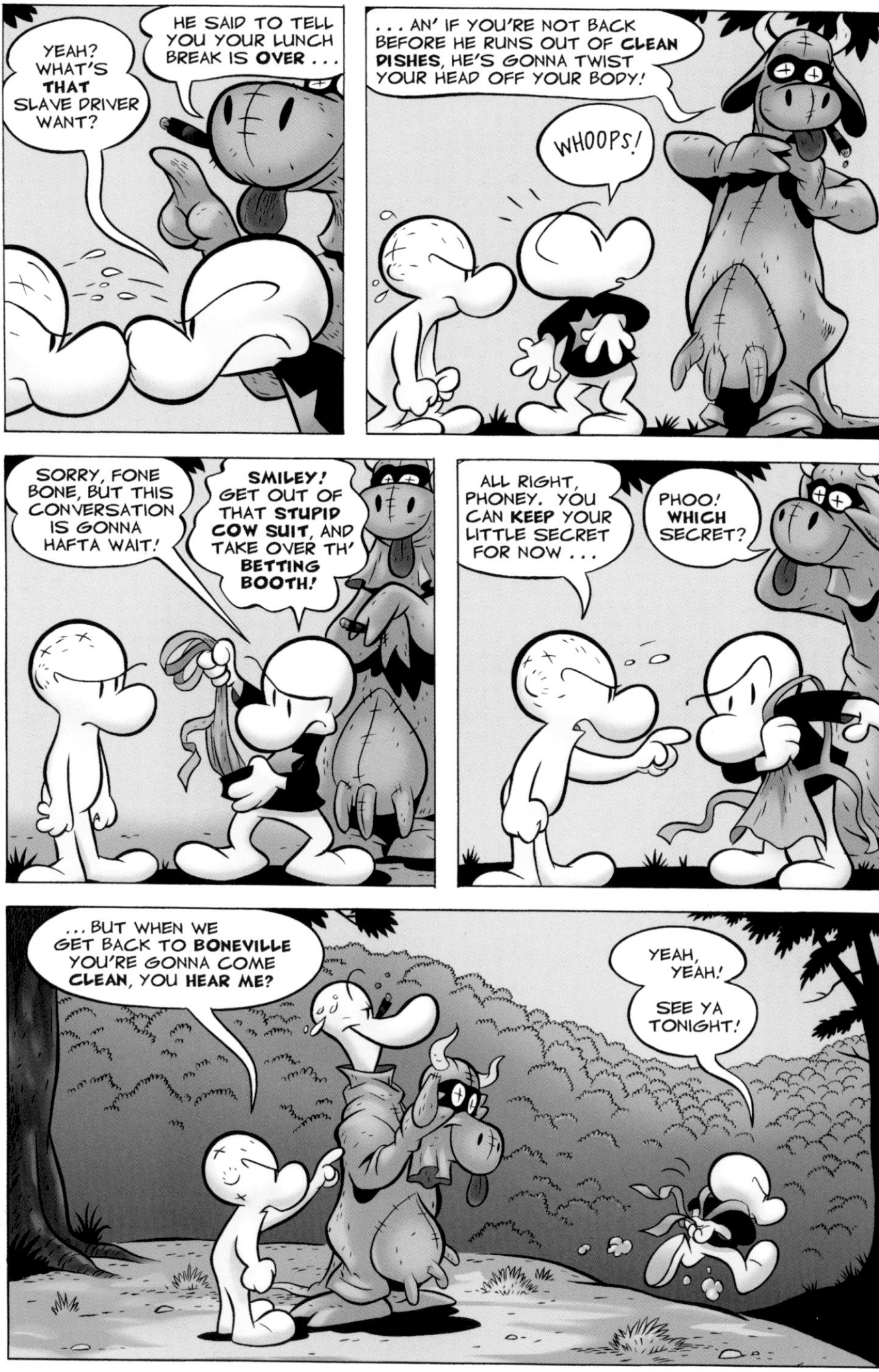
YEAH? WHAT'S **THAT** SLAVE DRIVER WANT?
HE SAID TO TELL YOU YOUR LUNCH BREAK IS **OVER** . . .
. . . AN' IF YOU'RE NOT BACK BEFORE HE RUNS OUT OF **CLEAN DISHES**, HE'S GONNA TWIST YOUR HEAD OFF YOUR BODY!
WHOOPS!
SORRY, FONE BONE, BUT THIS CONVERSATION IS GONNA HAFTA WAIT!
SMILEY! GET OUT OF THAT **STUPID COW SUIT**, AND TAKE OVER TH' **BETTING BOOTH!**
ALL RIGHT, PHONEY. YOU CAN **KEEP** YOUR LITTLE SECRET FOR NOW . . .
PHOO! **WHICH** SECRET?
. . . BUT WHEN WE GET BACK TO **BONEVILLE** YOU'RE GONNA COME **CLEAN**, YOU **HEAR ME?**
YEAH, YEAH!
SEE YA TONIGHT!

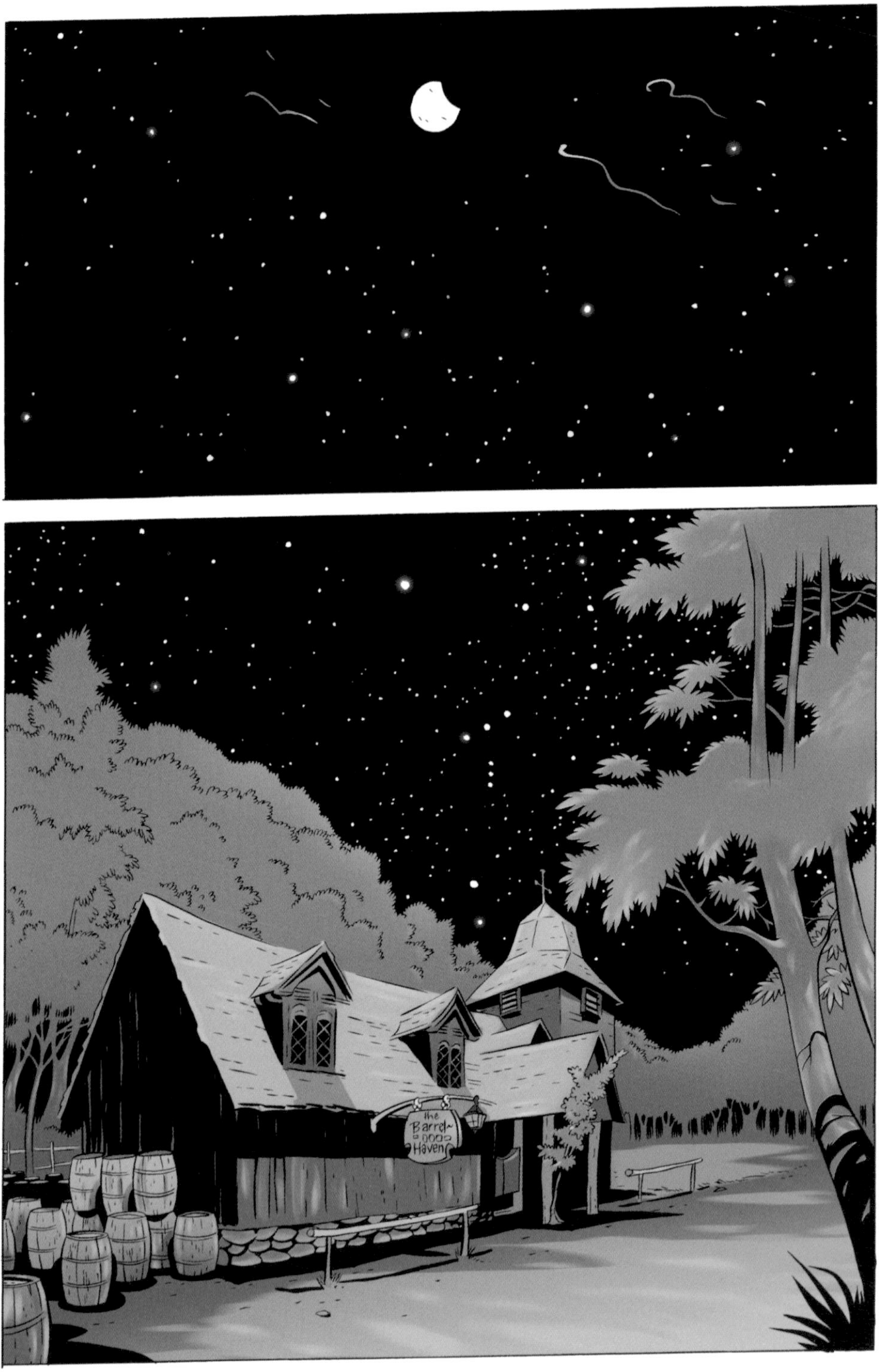
the Barrel Haven

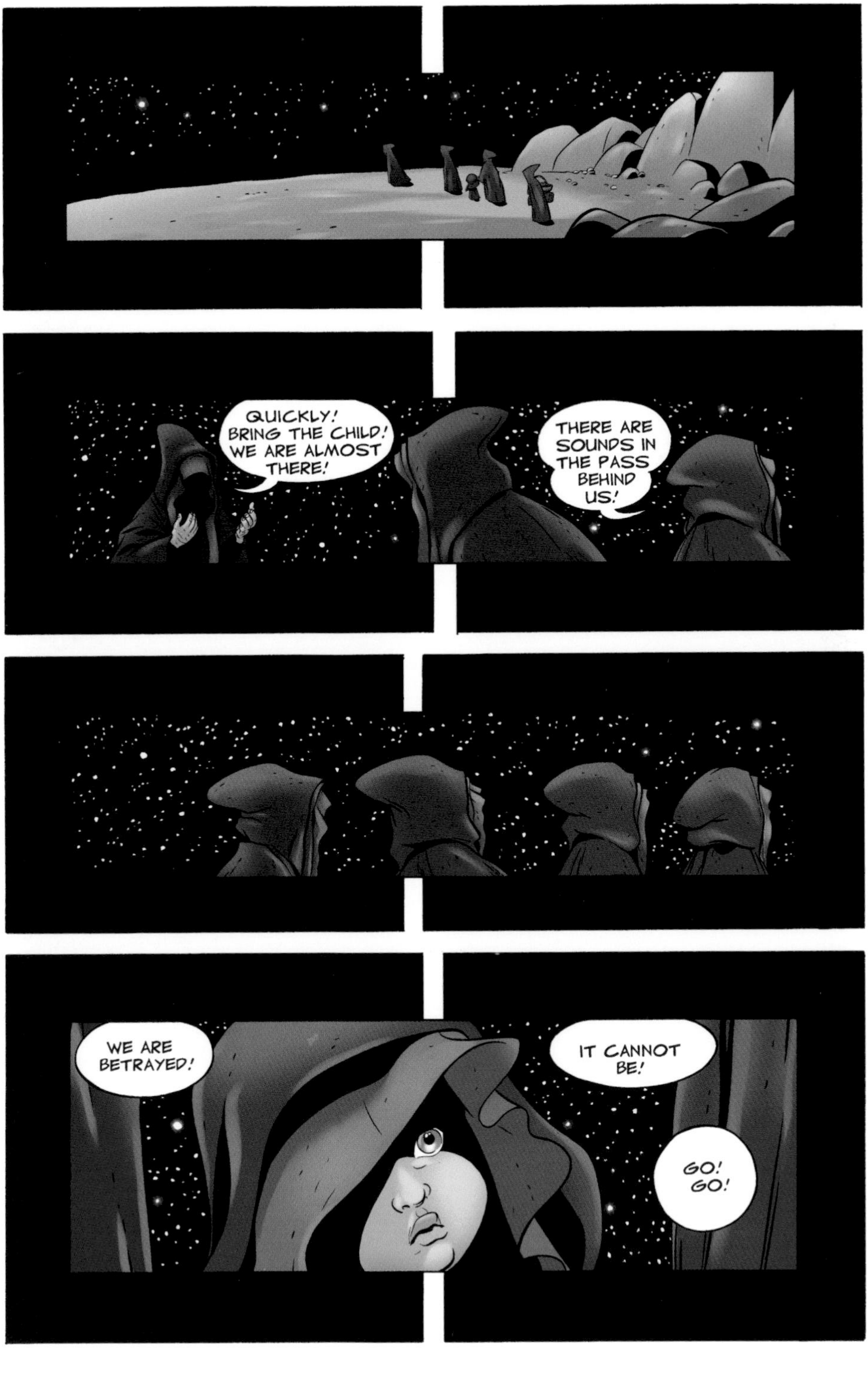
QUICKLY! BRING THE CHILD! WE ARE ALMOST THERE!
THERE ARE SOUNDS IN THE PASS BEHIND US!
WE ARE BETRAYED!
IT CANNOT BE!
GO! GO!

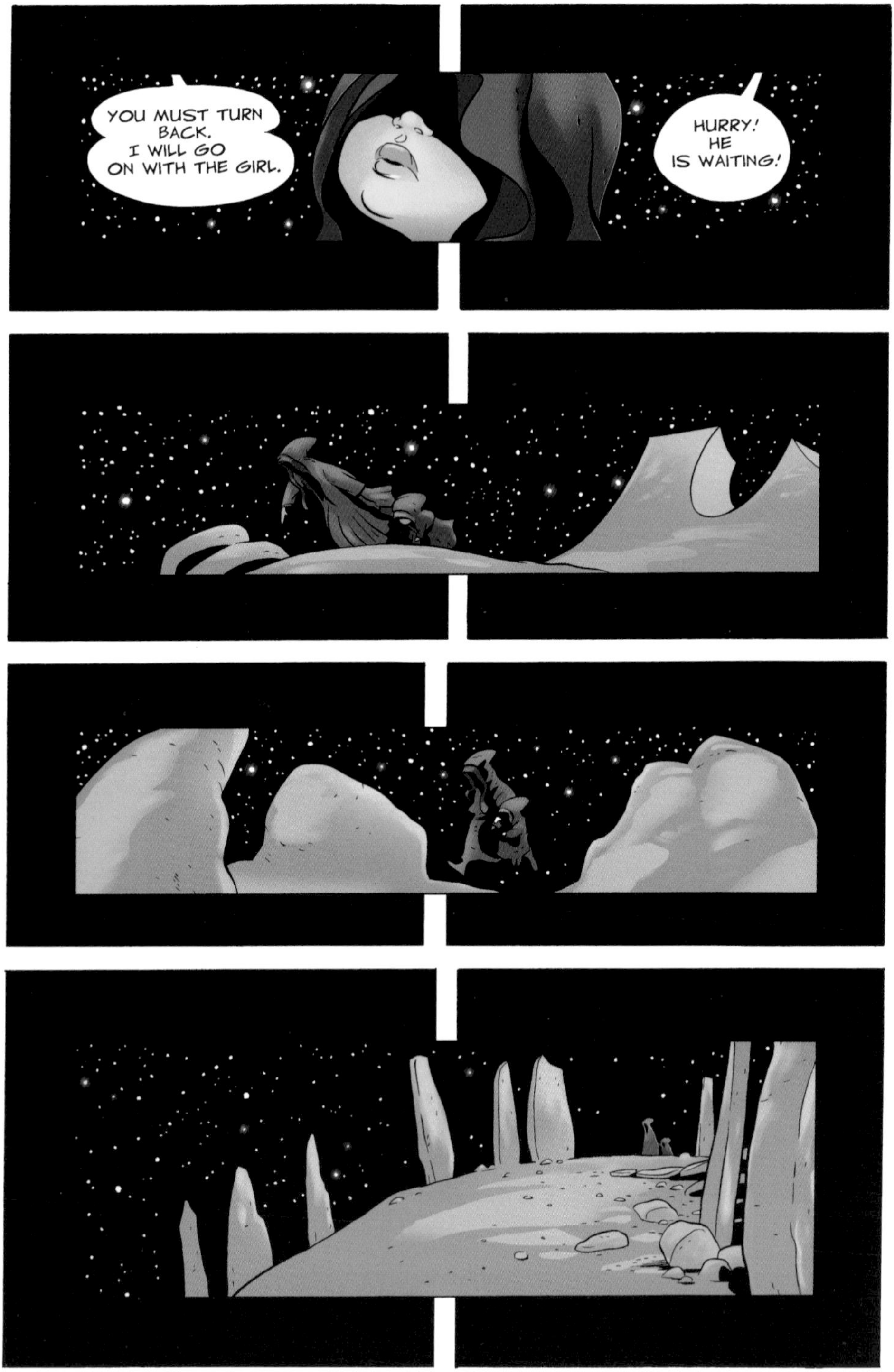
YOU MUST TURN BACK. I WILL GO ON WITH THE GIRL.
HURRY! HE IS WAITING!

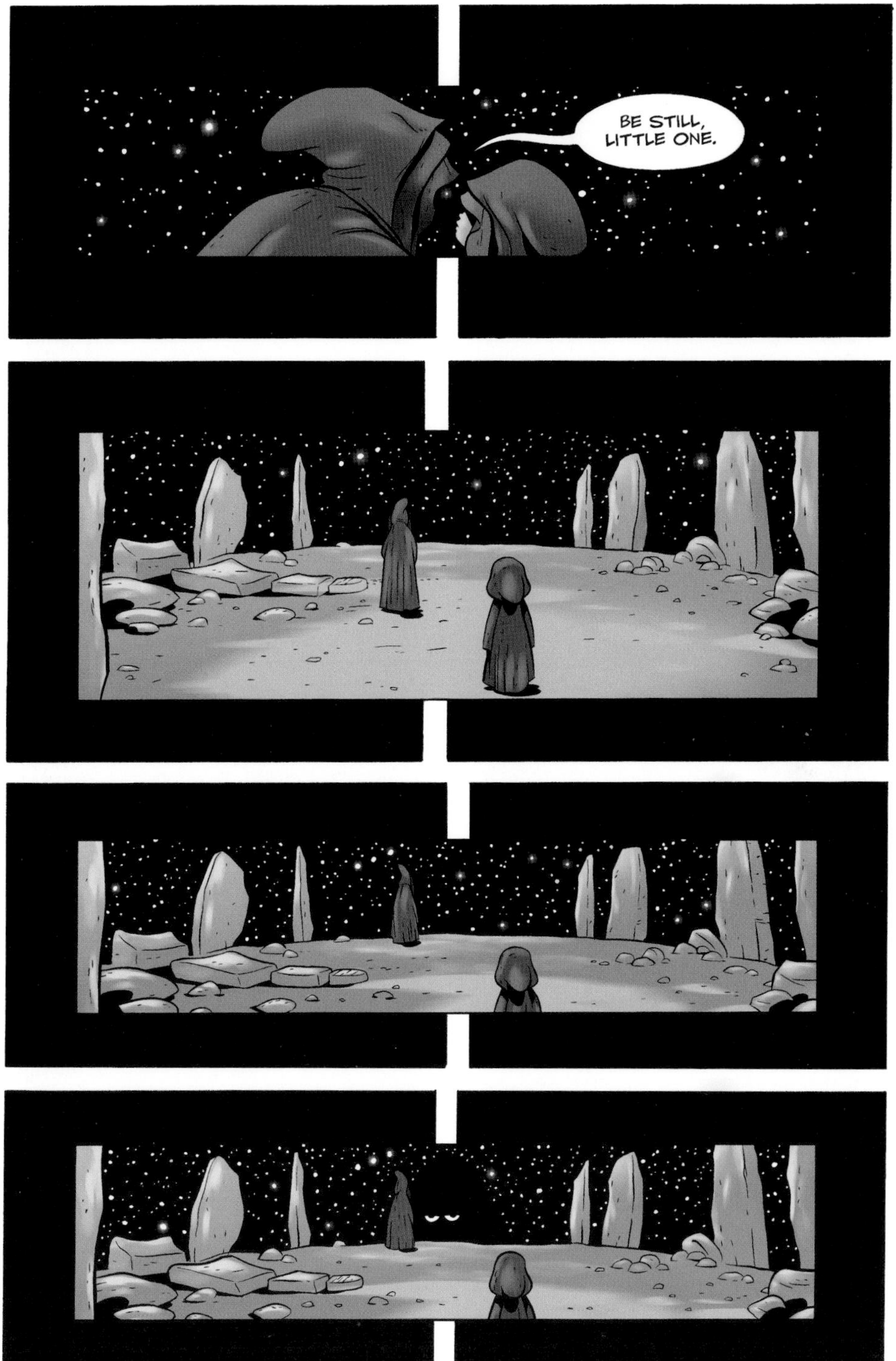
BE STILL, LITTLE ONE.

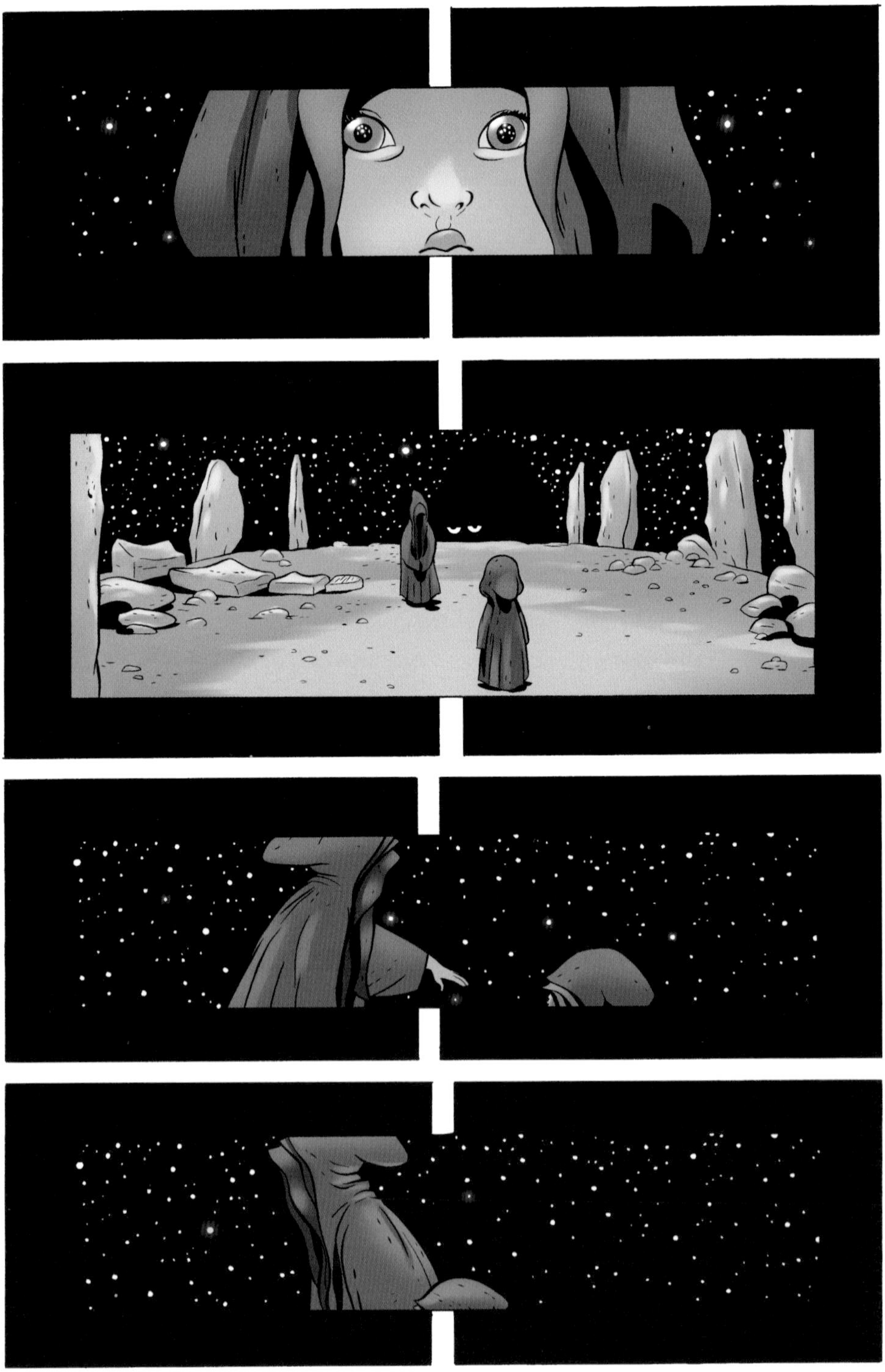

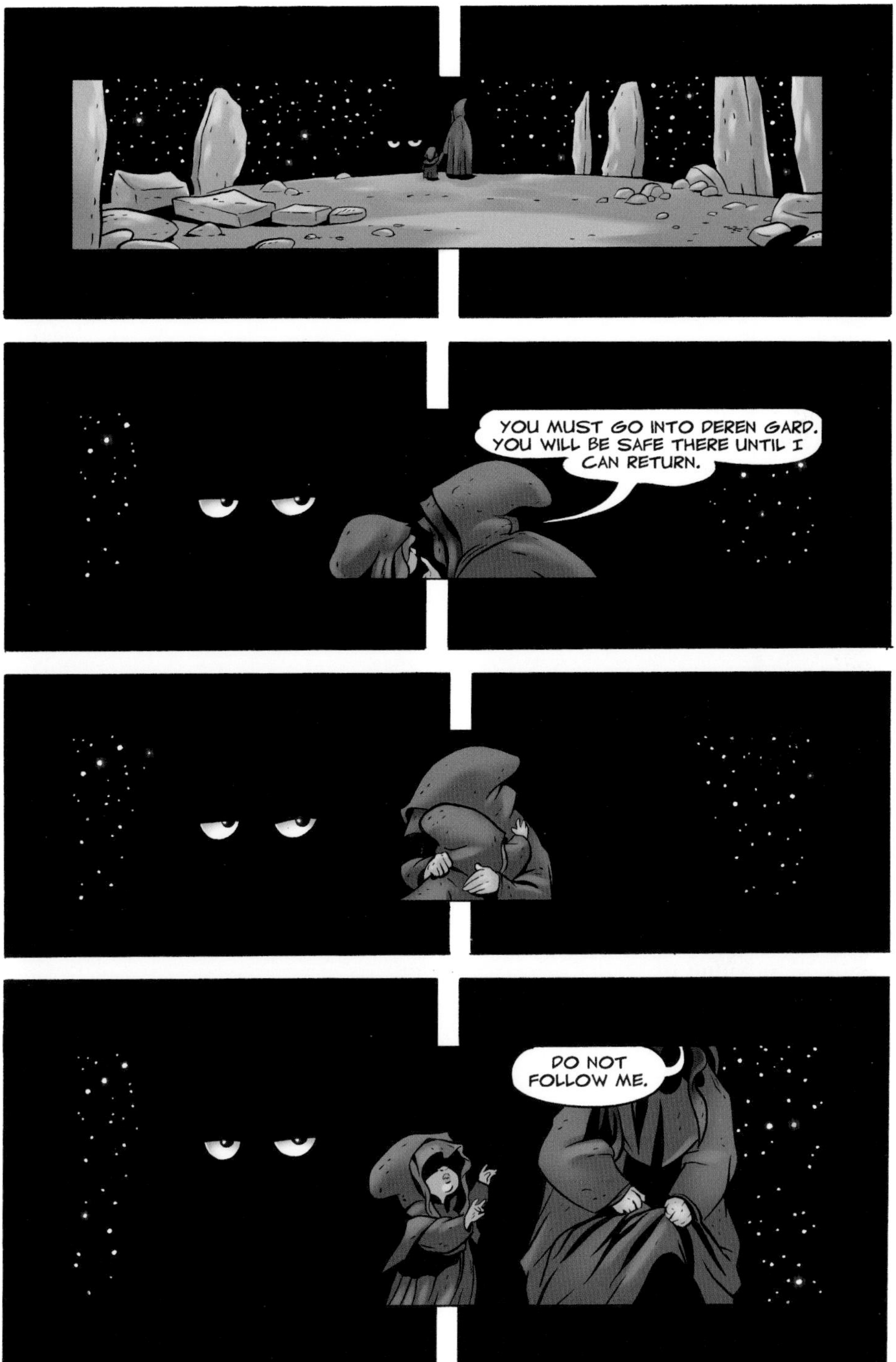
YOU MUST GO INTO DEREN GARD. YOU WILL BE SAFE THERE UNTIL I CAN RETURN.
DO NOT FOLLOW ME.

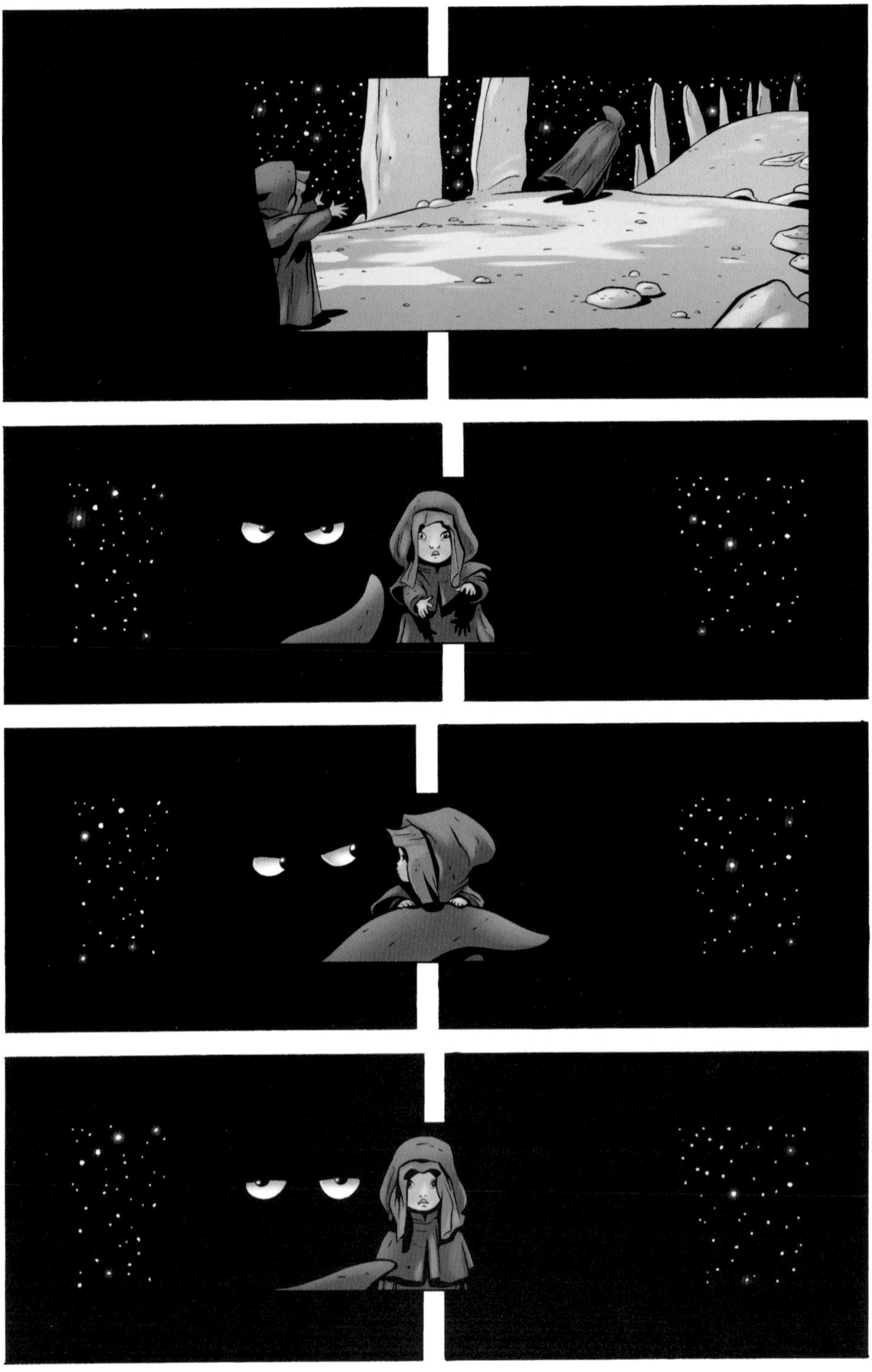

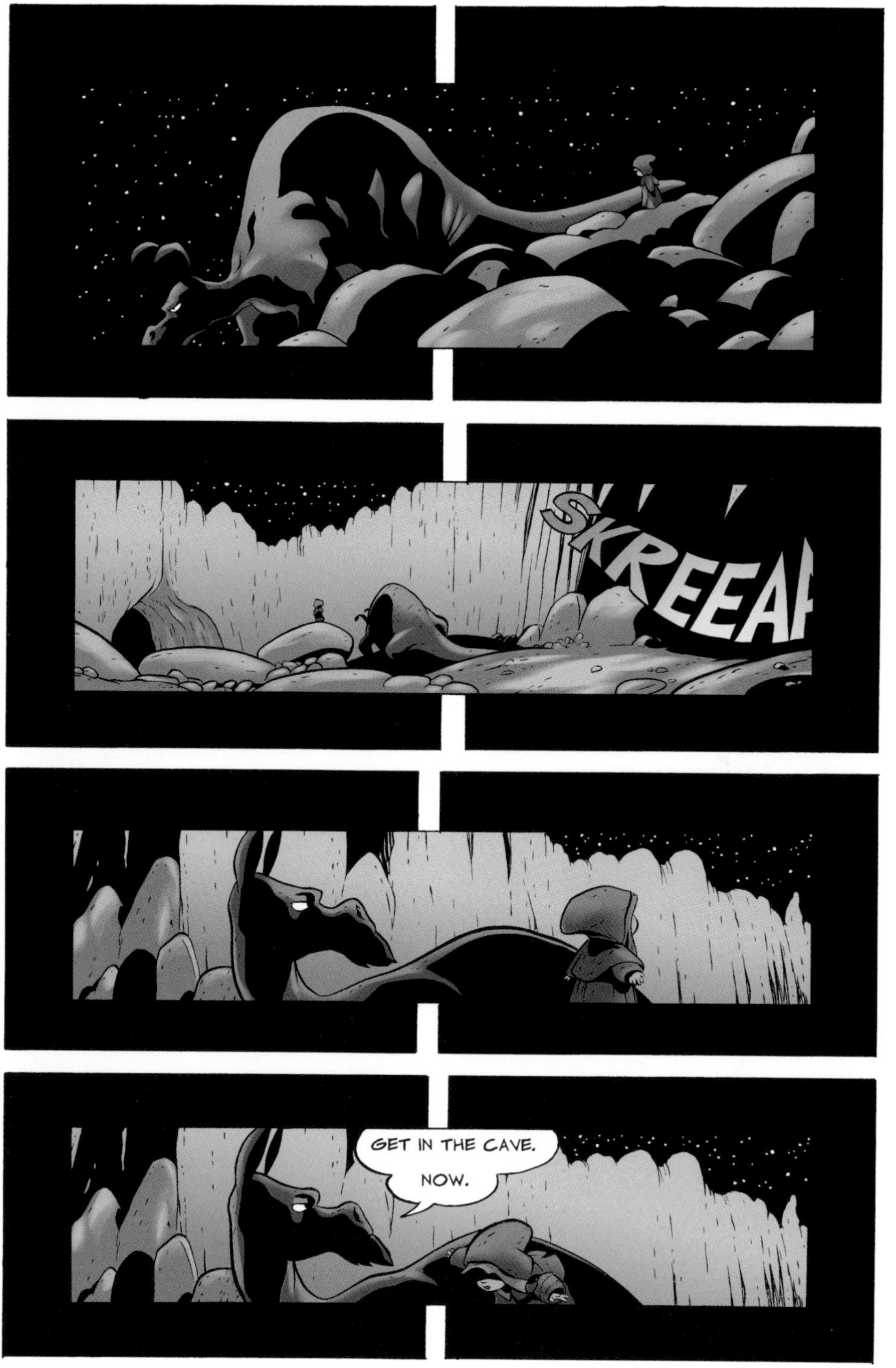
SKREEAR
GET IN THE CAVE.
NOW.

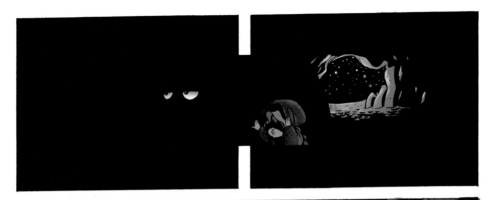

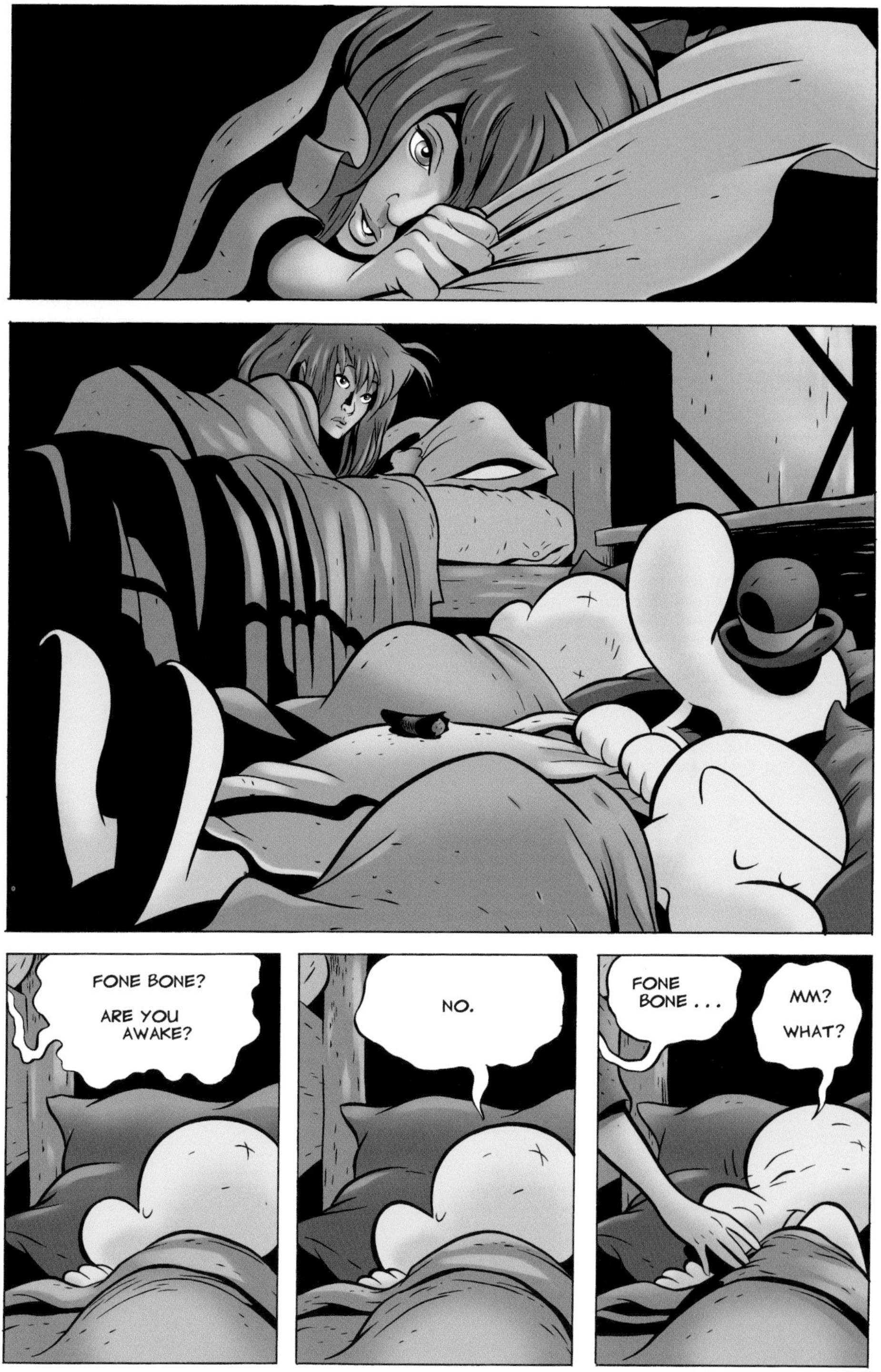
FONE BONE?
ARE YOU AWAKE?
NO.
FONE BONE . . .
MM?
WHAT?

KEEP YOUR VOICE DOWN.

WHAT IS IT, THORN? YOU HAVE ANOTHER WEIRD DREAM?

YES.

. . . GET UP, BUT DON'T WAKE THE OTHERS.

OKAY.

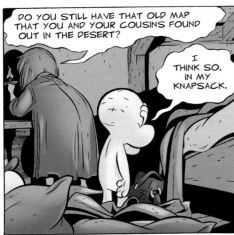

DO YOU STILL HAVE THAT OLD MAP THAT YOU AND YOUR COUSINS FOUND OUT IN THE DESERT?

I THINK SO. IN MY KNAPSACK.

HERE IT IS. YOU KNOW . . . WHEN I WAS **LOST** OUT IN TH' DESERT, I ACTUALLY **FOLLOWED** THIS MAP INTO TH' VALLEY!

LET'S SIT AT THE TABLE.

WHEN I WAS A LITTLE GIRL, I USED TO HAVE THIS **ONE** DREAM **OVER** AND **OVER** AGAIN. IN THE DREAM I WAS STANDING IN A **MAGNIFICENT CAVERN -- SURROUNDED** BY **DRAGONS!**

AND NOW YOU'RE STARTING TO HAVE THIS DREAM AGAIN?

YES. AND WHENEVER I **HAVE** IT, IT WAKES ME UP IN THE MIDDLE OF THE NIGHT.

HAVE YOU TOLD GRAN'MA BEN ABOUT THE DREAMS?

YAWN!

I DID WHEN I WAS LITTLE. SHE USED TO TELL ME NOT TO BE AFRAID BECAUSE DRAGONS DON'T REALLY **EXIST!**

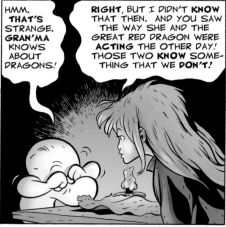

HMM. **THAT'S** STRANGE. **GRAN'MA** KNOWS ABOUT DRAGONS!

RIGHT, BUT I DIDN'T **KNOW** THAT THEN. AND YOU SAW THE WAY SHE AND THE GREAT RED DRAGON WERE **ACTING** THE OTHER DAY! THOSE TWO **KNOW** SOMETHING THAT WE **DON'T!**

YOU THINK IT HAS SOMETHING TO DO WITH THIS **MAP?**

ALL **I** KNOW IS I STOPPED HAVING THAT DREAM **YEARS** AGO - - UNTIL **YOU** SHOWED UP AND PULLED THAT MAP OUT OF YOUR KNAPSACK!

EVER SINCE THEN THE DREAMS HAVE BEEN BACK - - AND THEY'RE MORE **VIVID** AND **REAL** THAN **EVER BEFORE!**

I STILL DON'T UNDERSTAND WHY **SEEING** THIS OL' MAP WOULD TRIGGER TH' **DREAMS.**

I THINK **I DO** . . .

. . . I **DREW** THAT MAP!

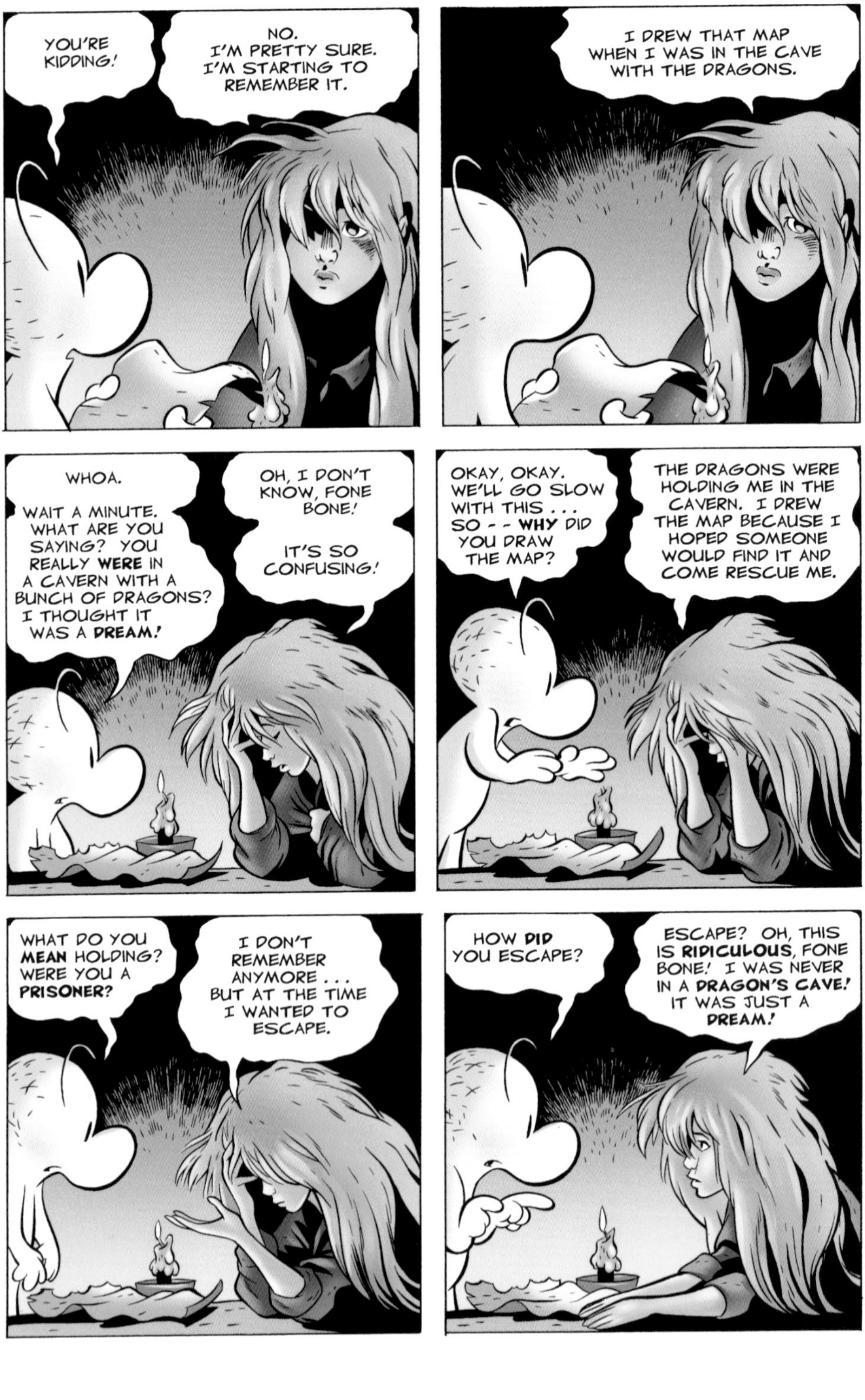
YOU'RE KIDDING!
NO. I'M PRETTY SURE. I'M STARTING TO REMEMBER IT.
I DREW THAT MAP WHEN I WAS IN THE CAVE WITH THE DRAGONS.
WHOA.
WAIT A MINUTE. WHAT ARE YOU SAYING? YOU REALLY WERE IN A CAVERN WITH A BUNCH OF DRAGONS? I THOUGHT IT WAS A DREAM!
OH, I DON'T KNOW, FONE BONE!
IT'S SO CONFUSING!
OKAY, OKAY. WE'LL GO SLOW WITH THIS . . . SO - - WHY DID YOU DRAW THE MAP?
THE DRAGONS WERE HOLDING ME IN THE CAVERN. I DREW THE MAP BECAUSE I HOPED SOMEONE WOULD FIND IT AND COME RESCUE ME.
WHAT DO YOU MEAN HOLDING? WERE YOU A PRISONER?
I DON'T REMEMBER ANYMORE . . . BUT AT THE TIME I WANTED TO ESCAPE.
HOW DID YOU ESCAPE?
ESCAPE? OH, THIS IS RIDICULOUS, FONE BONE! I WAS NEVER IN A DRAGON'S CAVE! IT WAS JUST A DREAM!

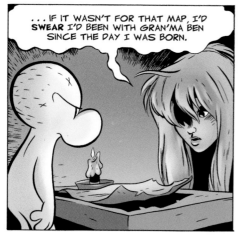

...IF IT WASN'T FOR THAT MAP, I'D **SWEAR** I'D BEEN WITH GRAN'MA BEN SINCE THE DAY I WAS BORN.

WELL, **THERE'S** TH' MAP! I SAY WE WAKE GRAN'MA UP AND **SHOW** IT TO HER!

NO. LET'S WAIT UNTIL AFTER THE RACE. SHE'S GOT ENOUGH TO WORRY ABOUT RIGHT NOW.

LET'S KEEP THE MAP A SECRET FOR NOW ...JUST BETWEEN YOU AND ME, OKAY?

OKAY. IF THAT'S WHAT YOU WANT.

GOOD. LET'S GO BACK TO BED.

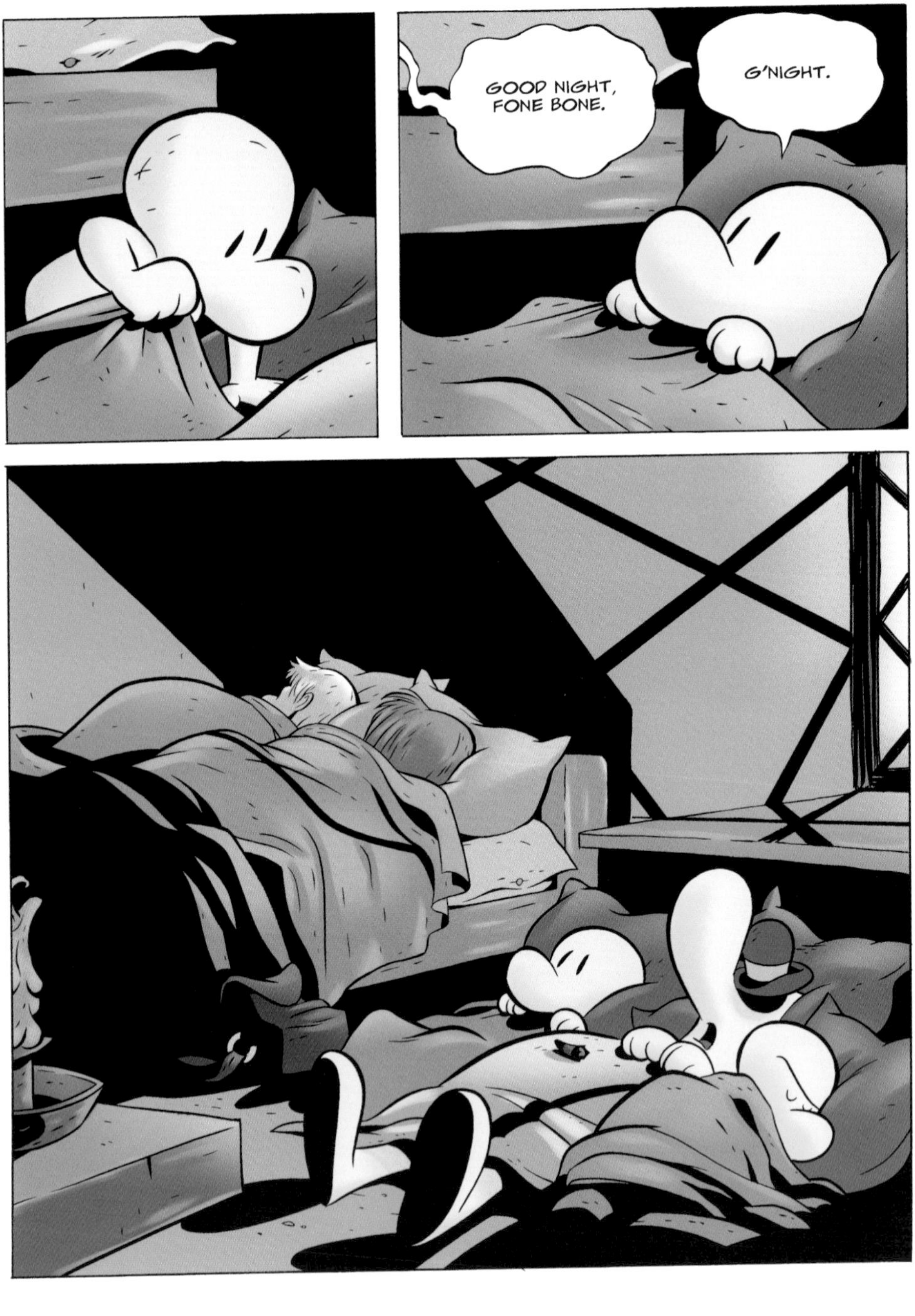
GOOD NIGHT, FONE BONE.
G'NIGHT.

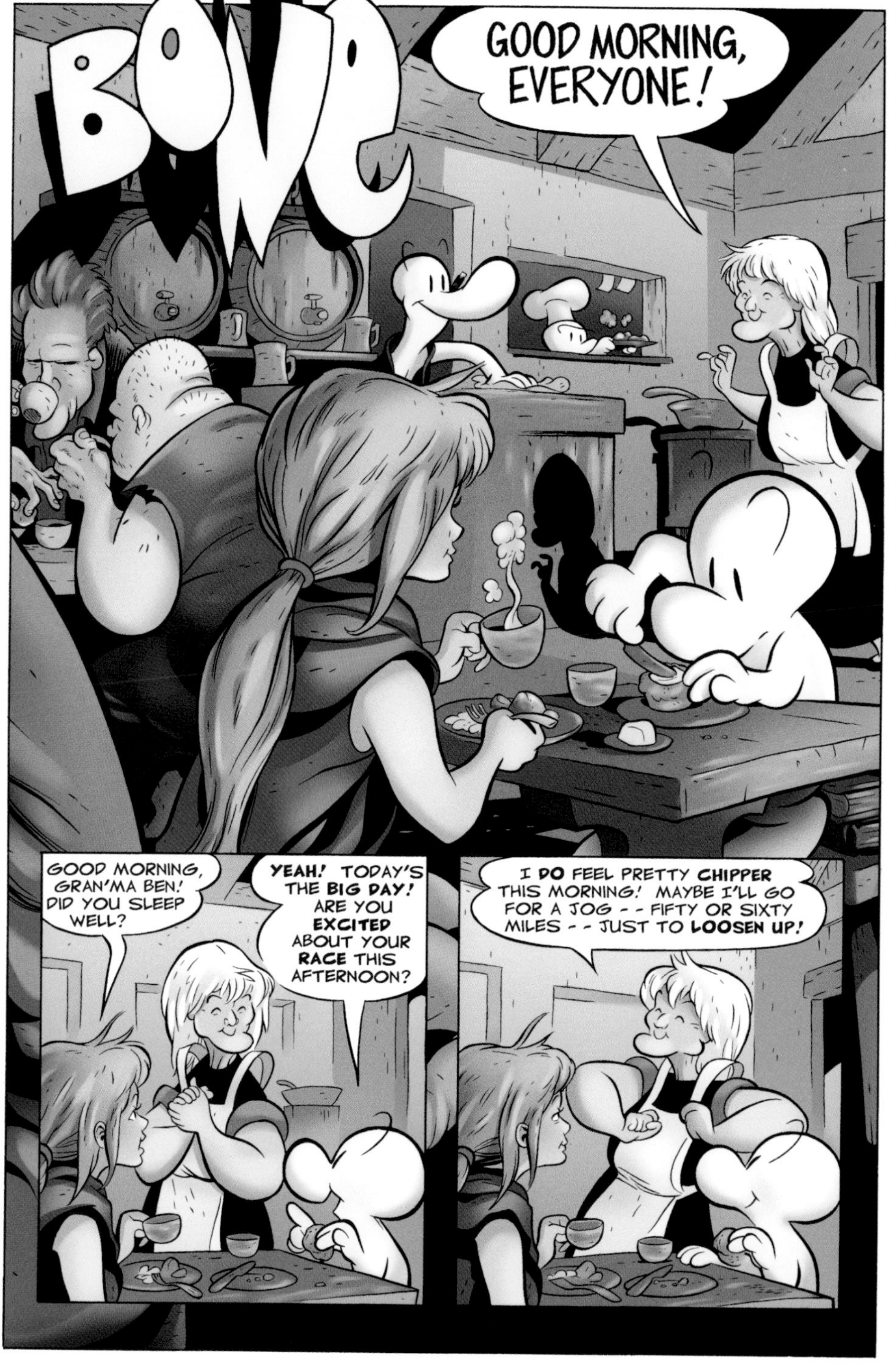
BONE
GOOD MORNING, EVERYONE!
GOOD MORNING, GRAN'MA BEN! DID YOU SLEEP WELL?
YEAH! TODAY'S THE BIG DAY! ARE YOU EXCITED ABOUT YOUR RACE THIS AFTERNOON?
I DO FEEL PRETTY CHIPPER THIS MORNING! MAYBE I'LL GO FOR A JOG - - FIFTY OR SIXTY MILES - - JUST TO LOOSEN UP!

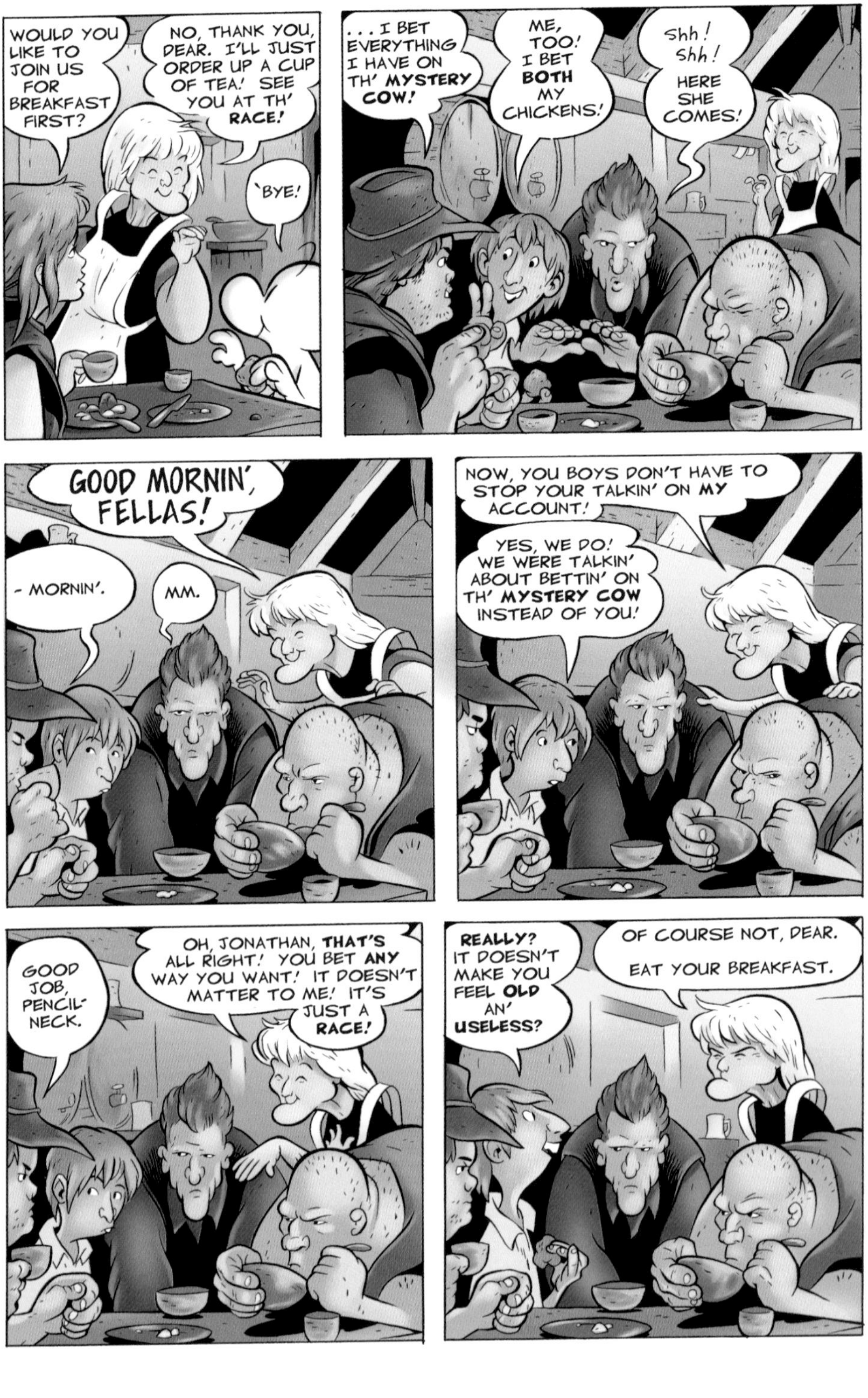
WOULD YOU LIKE TO JOIN US FOR BREAKFAST FIRST?
NO, THANK YOU, DEAR. I'LL JUST ORDER UP A CUP OF TEA! SEE YOU AT TH' RACE!
`BYE!
. . . I BET EVERYTHING I HAVE ON TH' MYSTERY COW!
ME, TOO! I BET BOTH MY CHICKENS!
Shh! Shh! HERE SHE COMES!
GOOD MORNIN', FELLAS!
- MORNIN'.
MM.
NOW, YOU BOYS DON'T HAVE TO STOP YOUR TALKIN' ON MY ACCOUNT!
YES, WE DO! WE WERE TALKIN' ABOUT BETTIN' ON TH' MYSTERY COW INSTEAD OF YOU!
GOOD JOB, PENCIL-NECK.
OH, JONATHAN, THAT'S ALL RIGHT! YOU BET ANY WAY YOU WANT! IT DOESN'T MATTER TO ME! IT'S JUST A RACE!
REALLY? IT DOESN'T MAKE YOU FEEL OLD AN' USELESS?
OF COURSE NOT, DEAR.
EAT YOUR BREAKFAST.

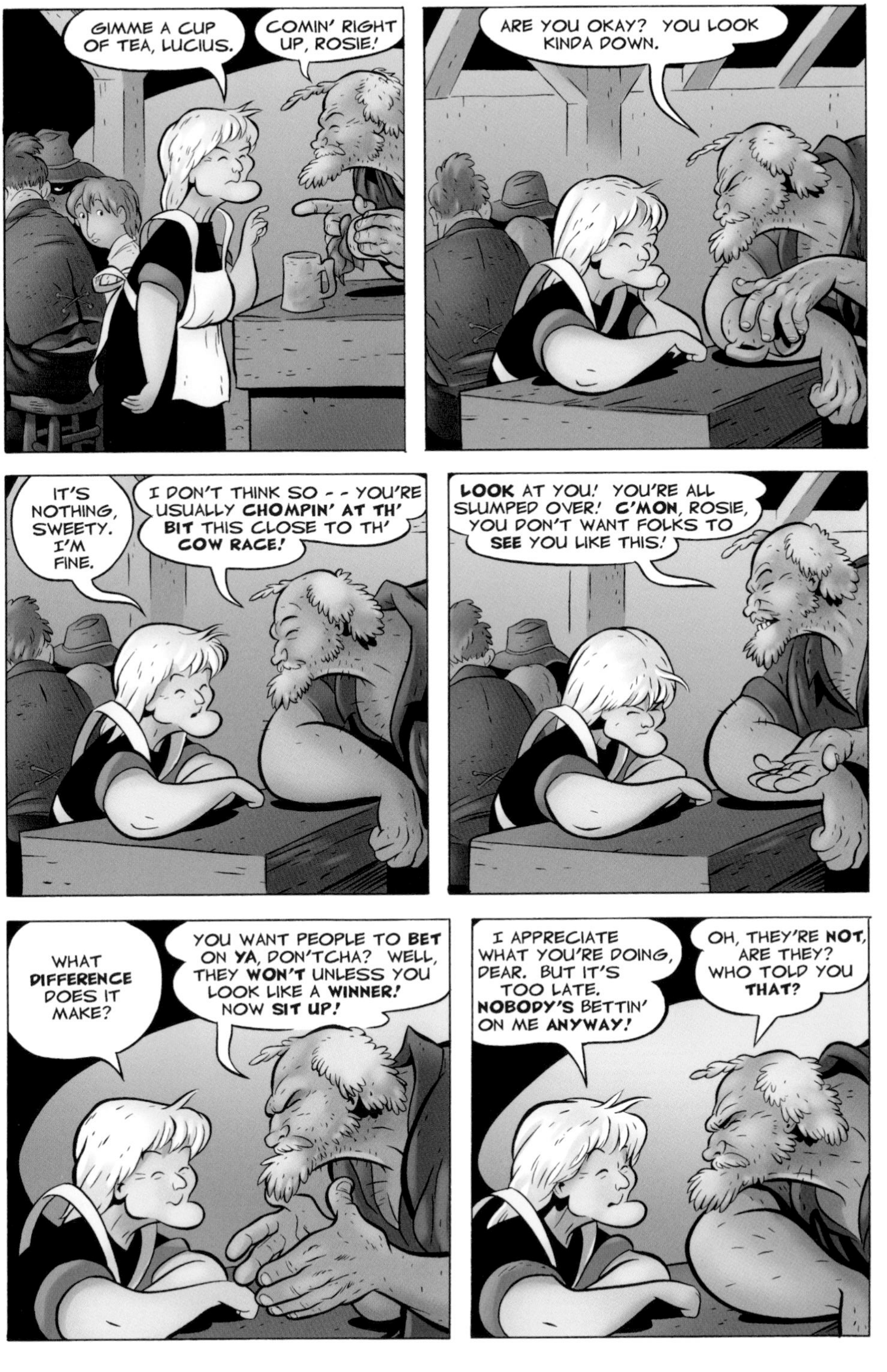
GIMME A CUP OF TEA, LUCIUS.
COMIN' RIGHT UP, ROSIE!
ARE YOU OKAY? YOU LOOK KINDA DOWN.
IT'S NOTHING, SWEETY. I'M FINE.
I DON'T THINK SO - - YOU'RE USUALLY **CHOMPIN' AT TH' BIT** THIS CLOSE TO TH' **COW RACE!**
LOOK AT YOU! YOU'RE ALL SLUMPED OVER! **C'MON**, ROSIE, YOU DON'T WANT FOLKS TO **SEE** YOU LIKE THIS!
WHAT **DIFFERENCE** DOES IT MAKE?
YOU WANT PEOPLE TO **BET** ON **YA**, DON'TCHA? WELL, THEY **WON'T** UNLESS YOU LOOK LIKE A **WINNER!** NOW **SIT UP!**
I APPRECIATE WHAT YOU'RE DOING, DEAR. BUT IT'S TOO LATE. **NOBODY'S** BETTIN' ON ME **ANYWAY!**
OH, THEY'RE **NOT**, ARE THEY? WHO TOLD YOU **THAT?**

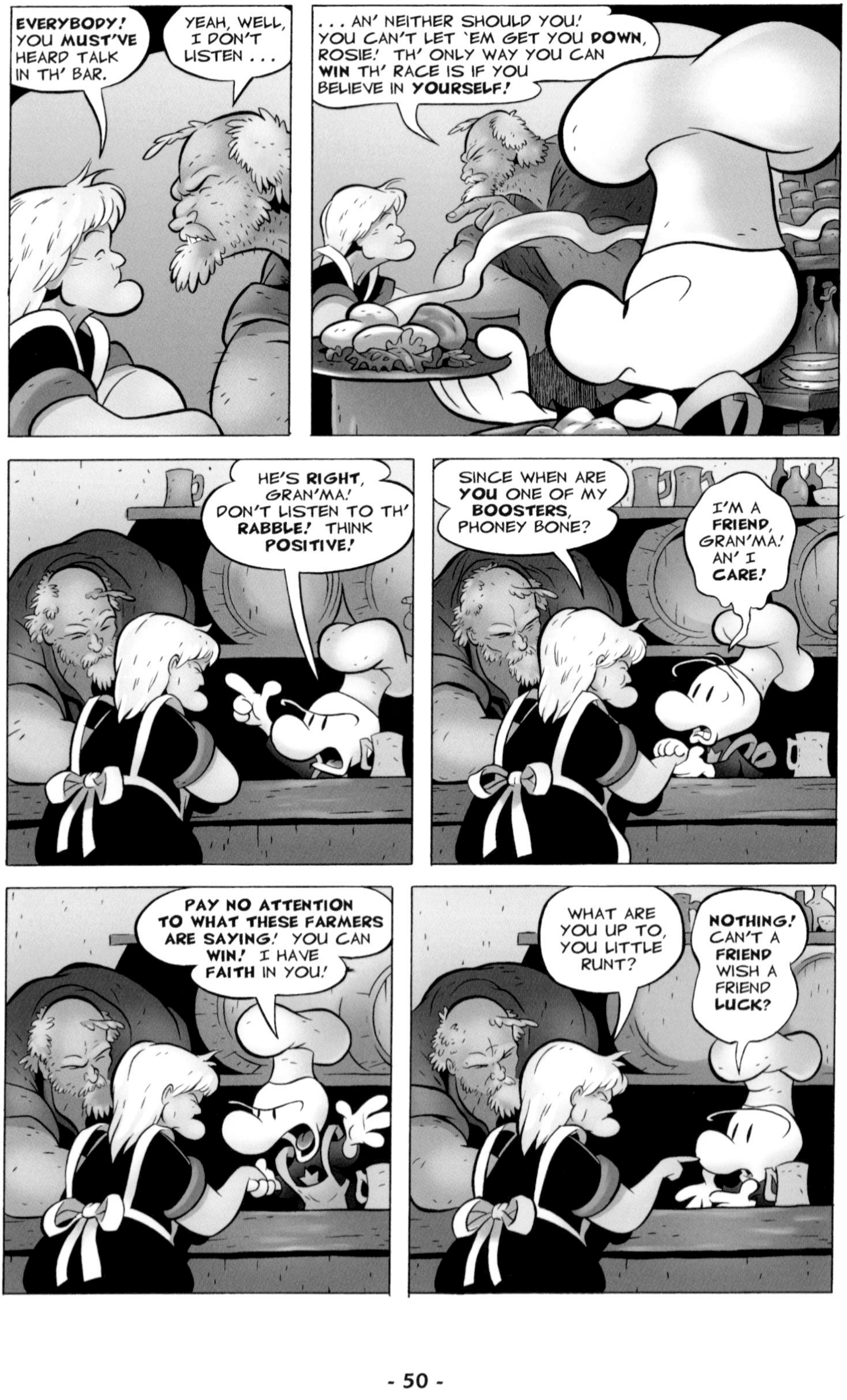
EVERYBODY! YOU MUST'VE HEARD TALK IN TH' BAR.
YEAH, WELL, I DON'T LISTEN . . .
. . . AN' NEITHER SHOULD YOU! YOU CAN'T LET 'EM GET YOU DOWN, ROSIE! TH' ONLY WAY YOU CAN WIN TH' RACE IS IF YOU BELIEVE IN YOURSELF!
HE'S RIGHT, GRAN'MA! DON'T LISTEN TO TH' RABBLE! THINK POSITIVE!
SINCE WHEN ARE YOU ONE OF MY BOOSTERS, PHONEY BONE?
I'M A FRIEND, GRAN'MA! AN' I CARE!
PAY NO ATTENTION TO WHAT THESE FARMERS ARE SAYING! YOU CAN WIN! I HAVE FAITH IN YOU!
WHAT ARE YOU UP TO, YOU LITTLE RUNT?
NOTHING! CAN'T A FRIEND WISH A FRIEND LUCK?

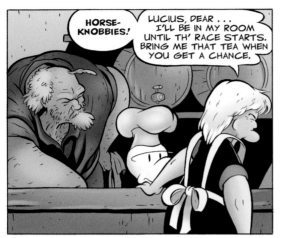

HORSE-KNOBBIES!

LUCIUS, DEAR . . . I'LL BE IN MY ROOM UNTIL TH' RACE STARTS. BRING ME THAT TEA WHEN YOU GET A CHANCE.

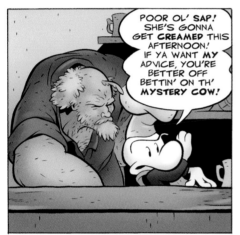

POOR OL' SAP! SHE'S GONNA GET CREAMED THIS AFTERNOON! IF YA WANT MY ADVICE, YOU'RE BETTER OFF BETTIN' ON TH' MYSTERY COW!

SPEAKING OF WHICH . . . A WELL-TO-DO MAN LIKE YOURSELF MUST BE THINKING OF MAKING A WAGER ON TH' RACE - - A REALLY, REALLY BIG WAGER! LIKE . . . OH, SAY . . . YOUR ENTIRE BAR!

. . . BUT THERE'S NO RUSH! WHEN YOU'RE READY TO BET - - YOU KNOW WHERE TO FIND ME! I'LL BE TAKING BETS RIGHT UP TO THE STARTING BELL! THINK ABOUT IT!

HMM.

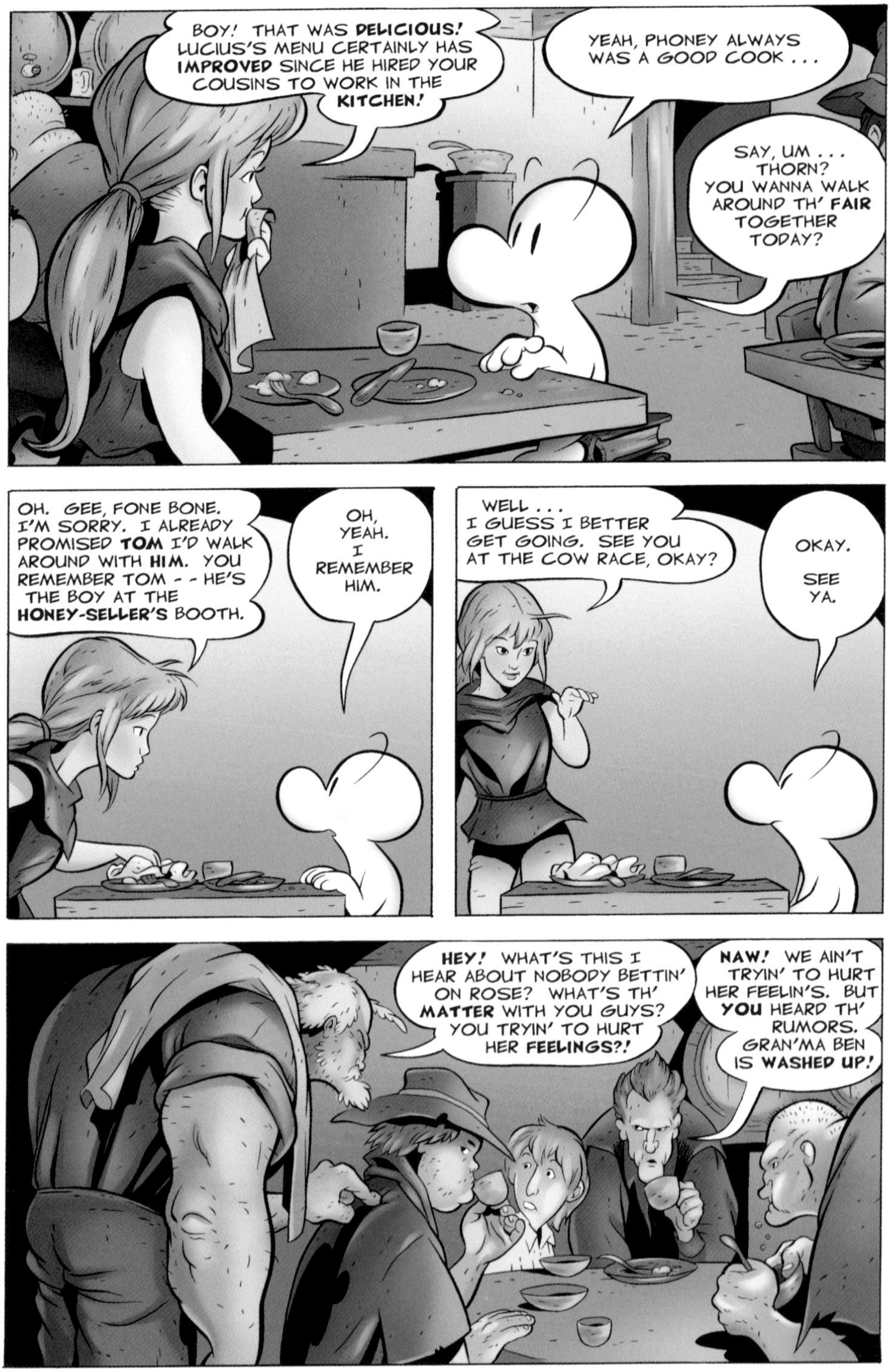
BOY! THAT WAS DELICIOUS! LUCIUS'S MENU CERTAINLY HAS IMPROVED SINCE HE HIRED YOUR COUSINS TO WORK IN THE KITCHEN!
YEAH, PHONEY ALWAYS WAS A GOOD COOK . . .
SAY, UM . . . THORN? YOU WANNA WALK AROUND TH' FAIR TOGETHER TODAY?
OH. GEE, FONE BONE. I'M SORRY. I ALREADY PROMISED TOM I'D WALK AROUND WITH HIM. YOU REMEMBER TOM - - HE'S THE BOY AT THE HONEY-SELLER'S BOOTH.
OH, YEAH. I REMEMBER HIM.
WELL . . . I GUESS I BETTER GET GOING. SEE YOU AT THE COW RACE, OKAY?
OKAY.
SEE YA.
HEY! WHAT'S THIS I HEAR ABOUT NOBODY BETTIN' ON ROSE? WHAT'S TH' MATTER WITH YOU GUYS? YOU TRYIN' TO HURT HER FEELINGS?!
NAW! WE AIN'T TRYIN' TO HURT HER FEELIN'S. BUT YOU HEARD TH' RUMORS. GRAN'MA BEN IS WASHED UP!

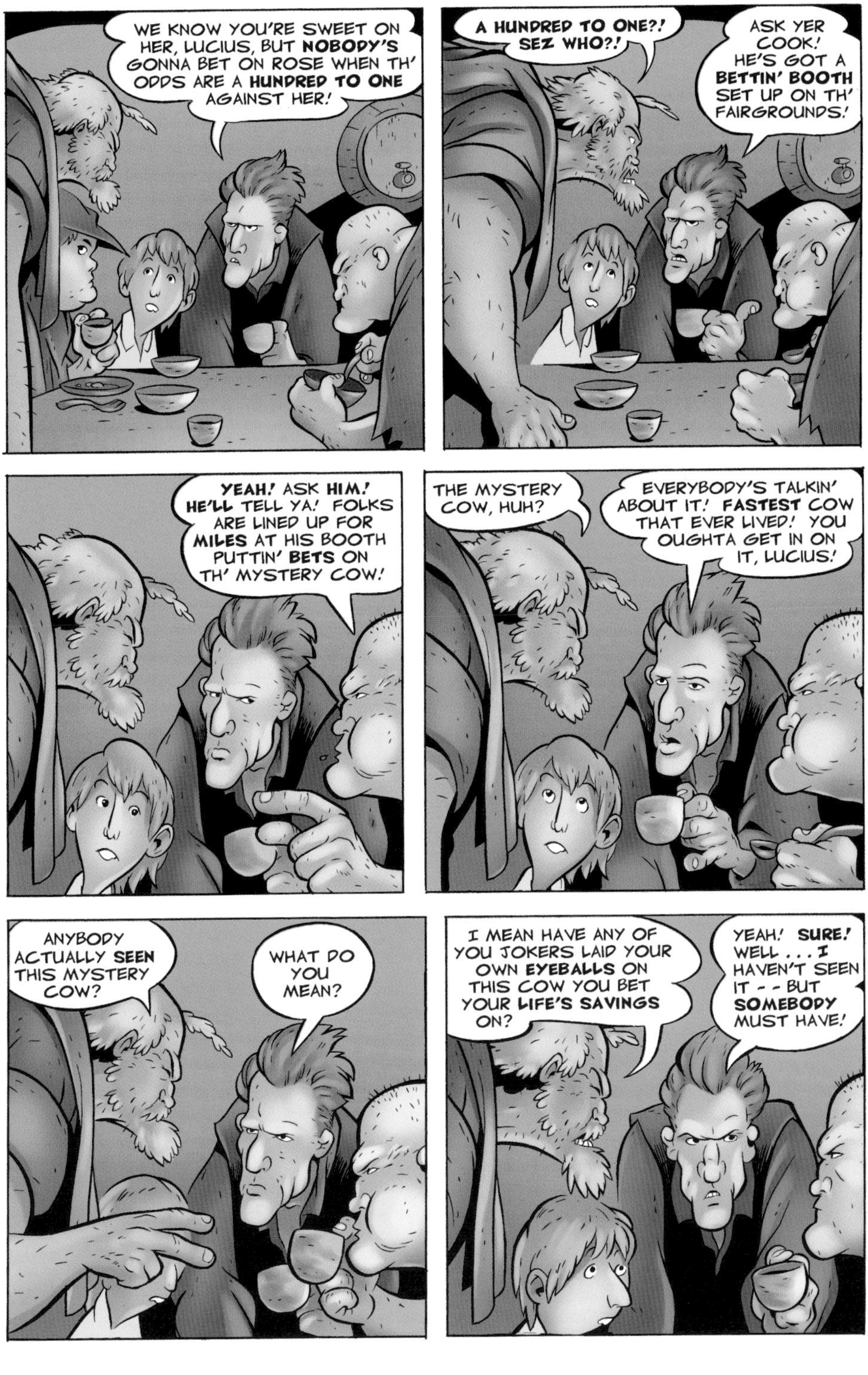
WE KNOW YOU'RE SWEET ON HER, LUCIUS, BUT NOBODY'S GONNA BET ON ROSE WHEN TH' ODDS ARE A HUNDRED TO ONE AGAINST HER!
A HUNDRED TO ONE?! SEZ WHO?!
ASK YER COOK! HE'S GOT A BETTIN' BOOTH SET UP ON TH' FAIRGROUNDS!
YEAH! ASK HIM! HE'LL TELL YA! FOLKS ARE LINED UP FOR MILES AT HIS BOOTH PUTTIN' BETS ON TH' MYSTERY COW!
THE MYSTERY COW, HUH?
EVERYBODY'S TALKIN' ABOUT IT! FASTEST COW THAT EVER LIVED! YOU OUGHTA GET IN ON IT, LUCIUS!
ANYBODY ACTUALLY SEEN THIS MYSTERY COW?
WHAT DO YOU MEAN?
I MEAN HAVE ANY OF YOU JOKERS LAID YOUR OWN EYEBALLS ON THIS COW YOU BET YOUR LIFE'S SAVINGS ON?
YEAH! SURE! WELL . . . I HAVEN'T SEEN IT - - BUT SOMEBODY MUST HAVE!

NOW, NOW, FELLAS! LET'S NOT GET EXCITED!

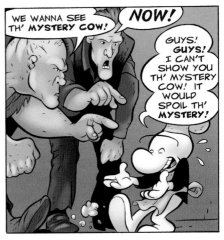

WE WANNA SEE TH' MYSTERY COW!

NOW!

GUYS! GUYS! I CAN'T SHOW YOU TH' MYSTERY COW! IT WOULD SPOIL TH' MYSTERY!

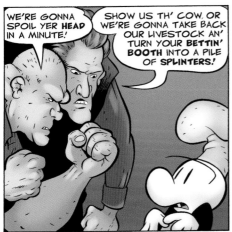

WE'RE GONNA SPOIL YER HEAD IN A MINUTE!

SHOW US TH' COW, OR WE'RE GONNA TAKE BACK OUR LIVESTOCK AN' TURN YOUR BETTIN' BOOTH INTO A PILE OF SPLINTERS!

OKAY, OKAY! I'LL TAKE YOU! BUT DON'T SAY I DIDN'T WARN YA! TH' MYSTERY COW IS TERRIBLE AN' DANGEROUS! I GOTTA MAKE SURE IT'S SAFE! GIMME TIL NOON -- THEN MEET ME AT TH' OL' LEANIN' BARN AT TH' EDGE OF TOWN!

YOU GOT TIL NOON, BALDY! AN' THIS BETTER BE ONE SCARY COW!

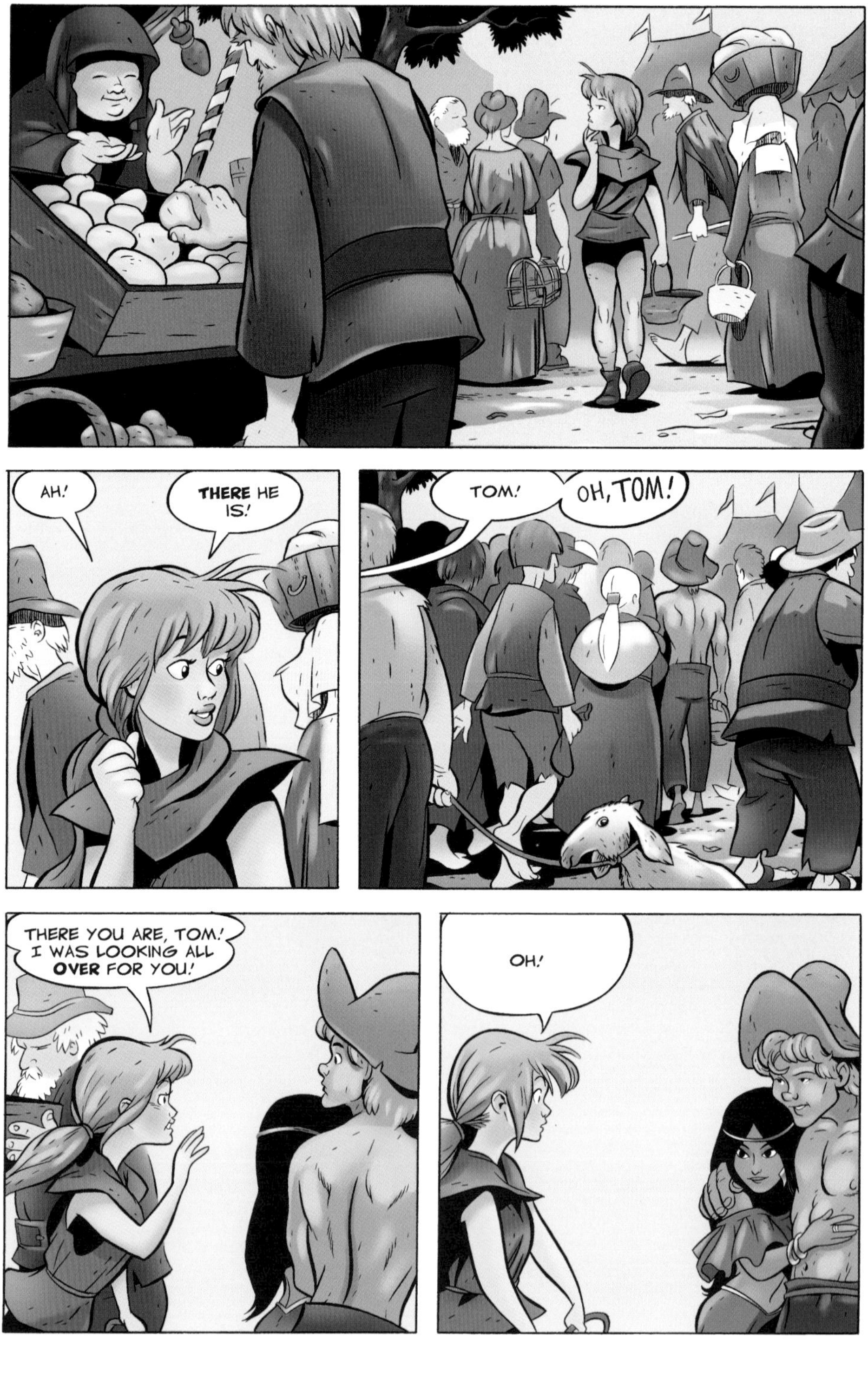
AH!
THERE HE IS!
TOM!
OH, TOM!
THERE YOU ARE, TOM! I WAS LOOKING ALL OVER FOR YOU!
OH!

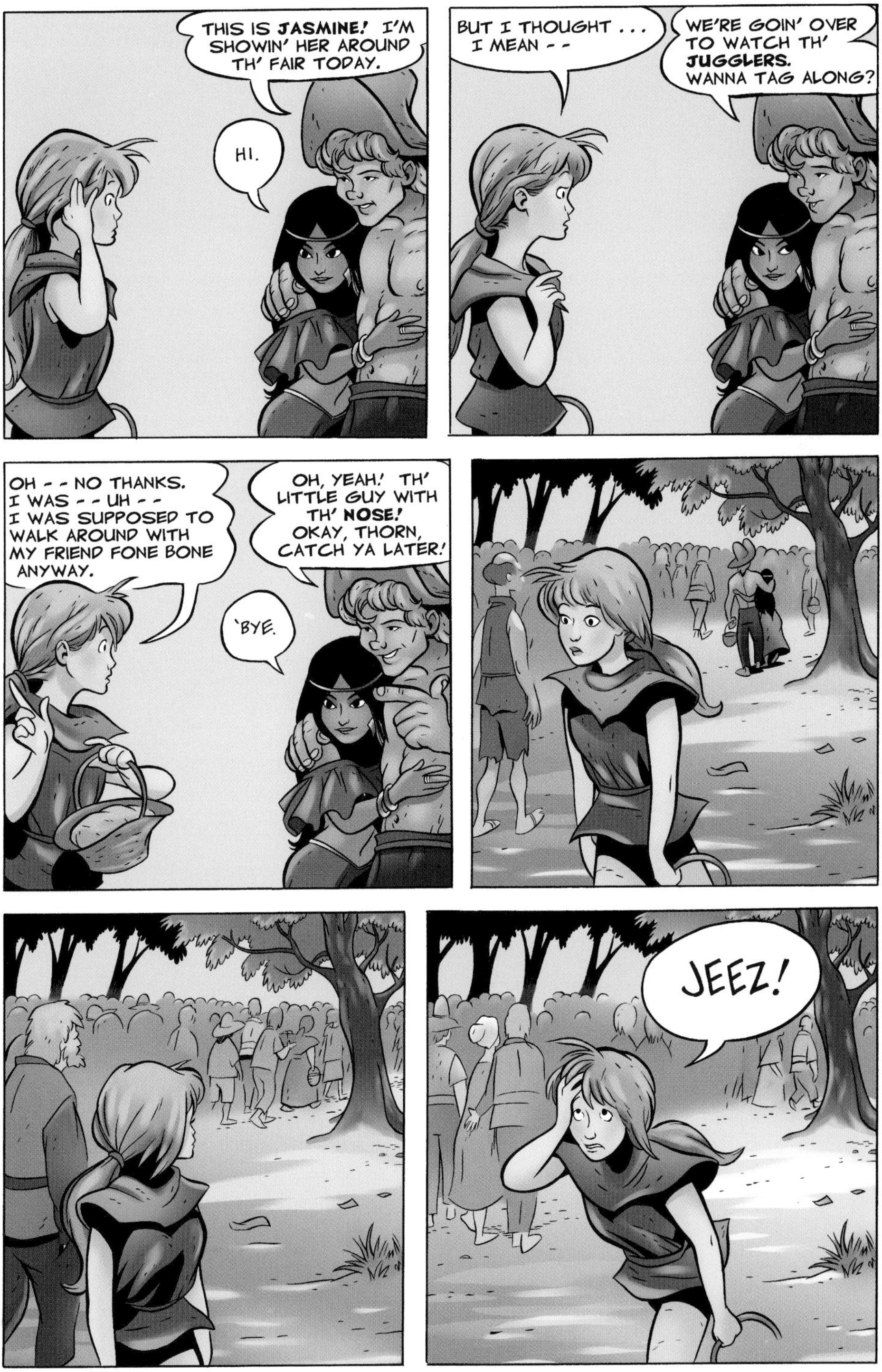
THIS IS **JASMINE!** I'M SHOWIN' HER AROUND TH' FAIR TODAY.
HI.
BUT I THOUGHT . . . I MEAN - -
WE'RE GOIN' OVER TO WATCH TH' **JUGGLERS.** WANNA TAG ALONG?
OH - - NO THANKS. I WAS - - UH - - I WAS SUPPOSED TO WALK AROUND WITH MY FRIEND FONE BONE ANYWAY.
OH, YEAH! TH' LITTLE GUY WITH TH' **NOSE!** OKAY, THORN, CATCH YA LATER!
'BYE.
JEEZ!

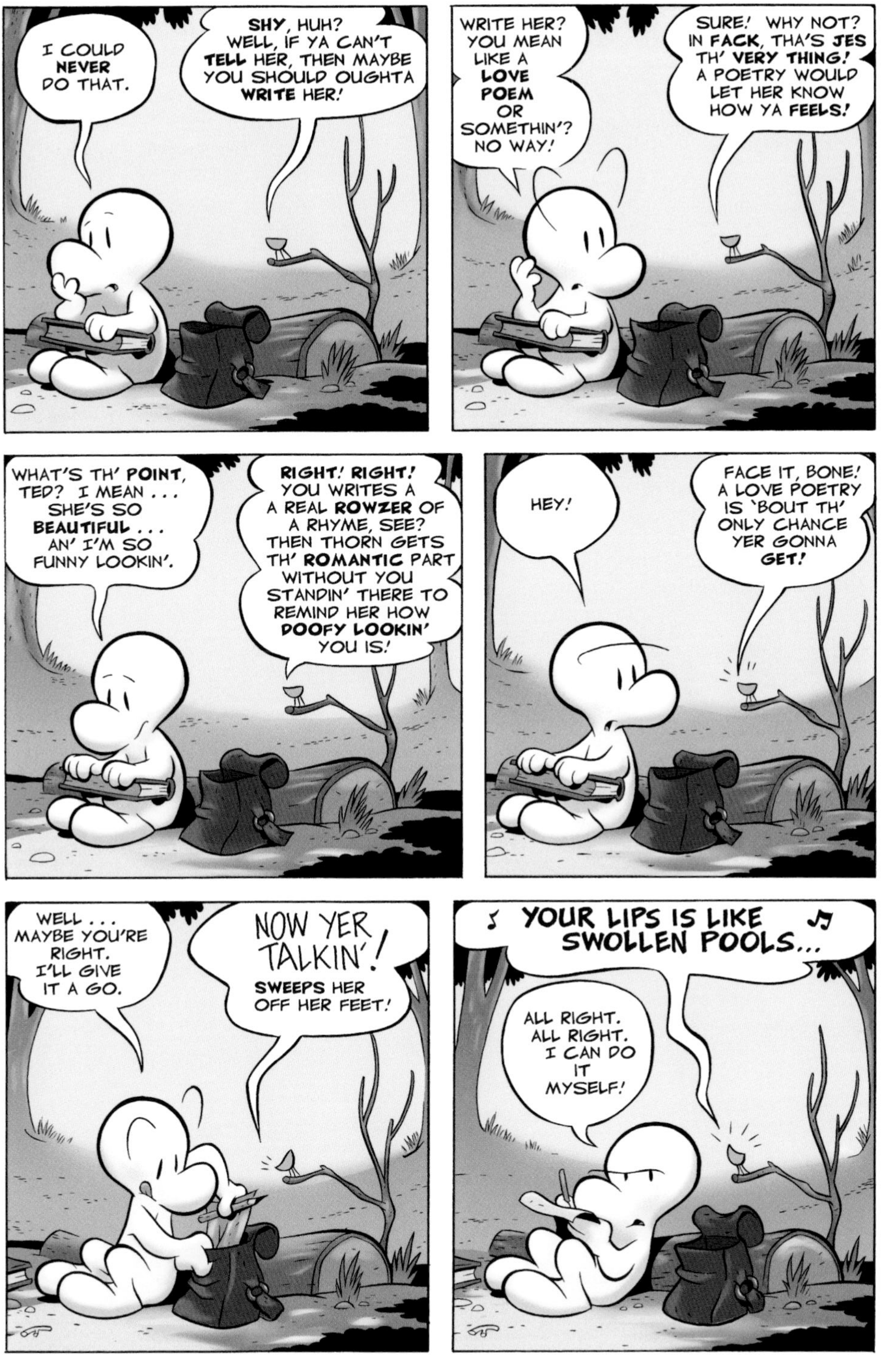
I COULD NEVER DO THAT.
SHY, HUH? WELL, IF YA CAN'T TELL HER, THEN MAYBE YOU SHOULD OUGHTA WRITE HER!
WRITE HER? YOU MEAN LIKE A LOVE POEM OR SOMETHIN'? NO WAY!
SURE! WHY NOT? IN FACK, THA'S JES TH' VERY THING! A POETRY WOULD LET HER KNOW HOW YA FEELS!
WHAT'S TH' POINT, TED? I MEAN . . . SHE'S SO BEAUTIFUL . . . AN' I'M SO FUNNY LOOKIN'.
RIGHT! RIGHT! YOU WRITES A A REAL ROWZER OF A RHYME, SEE? THEN THORN GETS TH' ROMANTIC PART WITHOUT YOU STANDIN' THERE TO REMIND HER HOW DOOFY LOOKIN' YOU IS!
HEY!
FACE IT, BONE! A LOVE POETRY IS 'BOUT TH' ONLY CHANCE YER GONNA GET!
WELL . . . MAYBE YOU'RE RIGHT. I'LL GIVE IT A GO.
NOW YER TALKIN'! SWEEPS HER OFF HER FEET!
YOUR LIPS IS LIKE SWOLLEN POOLS...
ALL RIGHT. ALL RIGHT. I CAN DO IT MYSELF!

THE MYSTERY COW

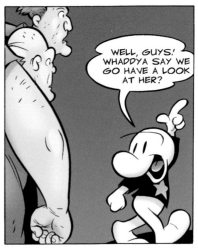

THE MYSTERY COW

GRAM!

GRAM, WAIT UP!

OH, HELLO, THORN! I'M ON MY WAY TO TH' STARTING LINE. I WANT TO GET A LOOK AT THIS **MYSTERY COW!**

WELL, DON'T WORRY ABOUT A THING! YOU'RE GOING TO DO FINE!

THANK YOU, SWEETY, BUT I BETTER GET GOING. IS MY NUMBER ON STRAIGHT?

IT'S STRAIGHT. HAVE YOU SEEN FONE BONE AROUND? I CAN'T FIND HIM **ANYWHERE!**

NOT SINCE BREAKFAST.

WISH ME LUCK, DEAR!

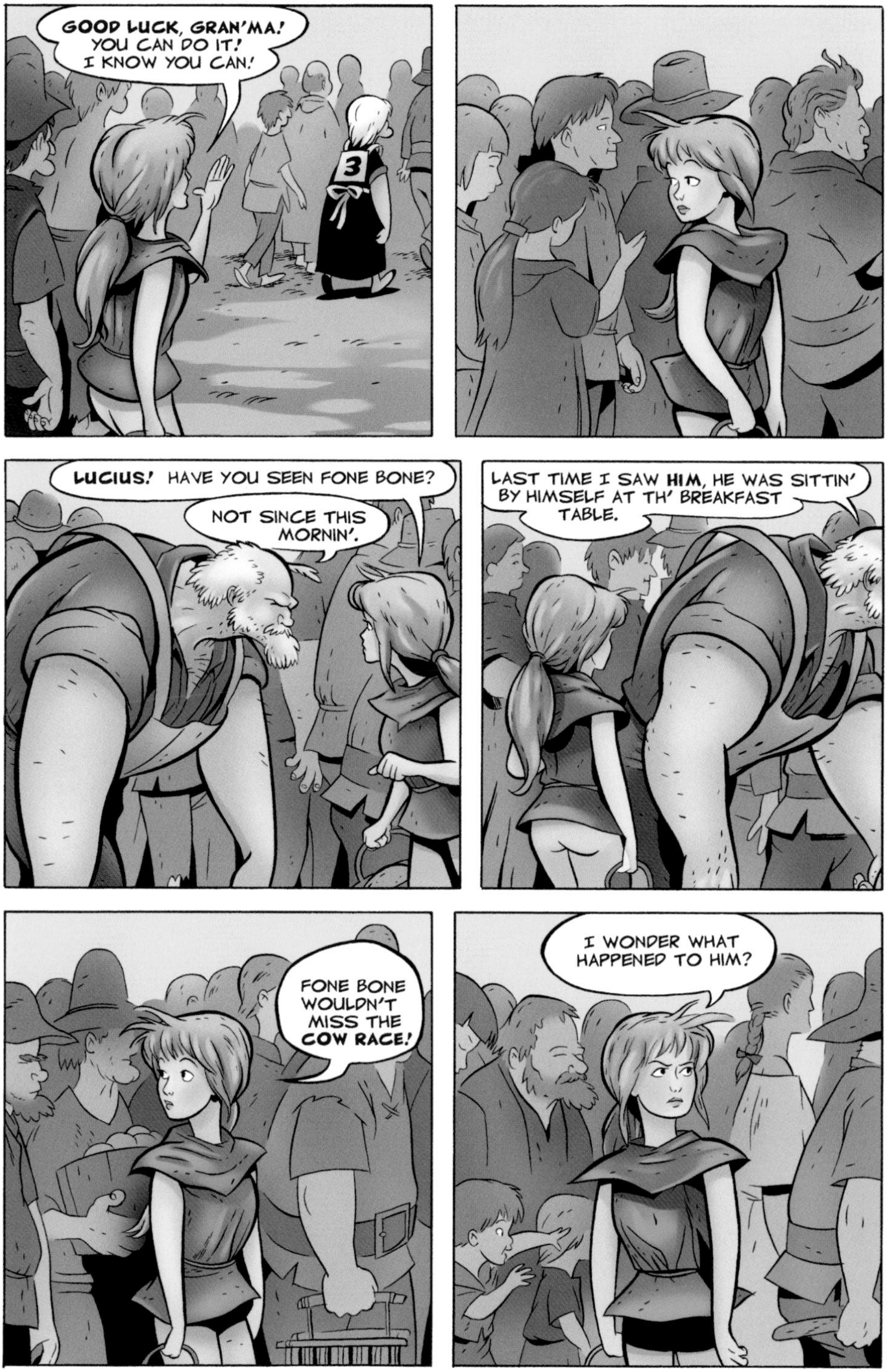
GOOD LUCK, GRAN'MA! YOU CAN DO IT! I KNOW YOU CAN!
LUCIUS! HAVE YOU SEEN FONE BONE?
NOT SINCE THIS MORNIN'.
LAST TIME I SAW HIM, HE WAS SITTIN' BY HIMSELF AT TH' BREAKFAST TABLE.
FONE BONE WOULDN'T MISS THE COW RACE!
I WONDER WHAT HAPPENED TO HIM?

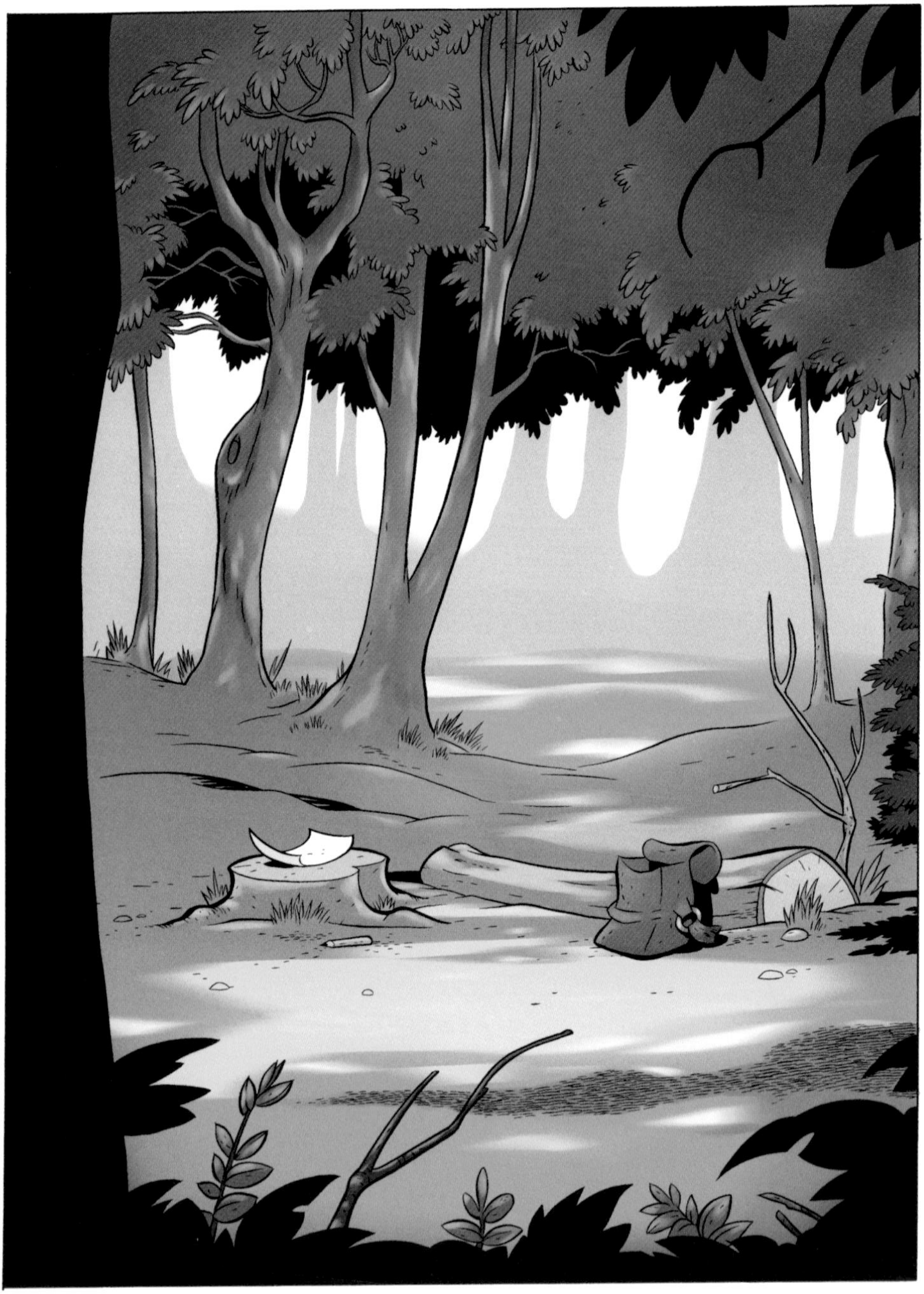

YEP. I'M HERE TO BET!

YEH. YEH. IS IT A BIG BET?

OH, YEAH, A REAL, BIG BET! I'M SHOOTIN' TH' WORKS!

≈ GASP! ≈ ARE YOU BETTIN' TH' BARREL-HAVEN?

FEAST YER EYES, BONE! THIS IS MY MARKER FOR TH' BARRELHAVEN TAVERN . . .

YES!

AN' I'M BETTIN' IT ALL ON GRAN'MA BEN TO WIN!!

WHAT?!

SMACK!

I UNDERSTAND TH' PAYOFF IS A HUNDRED TO ONE! SEE YA IN TH' WINNER'S CIRCLE!

BINK!

BAM! Your here

Place your bets here

AN' FOR YOUR SAKE, . . . OL' BUDDY . . . YOU BETTER HAVE TH' FUNDS TO COVER THAT BET!

Place your bets here

CLOSED

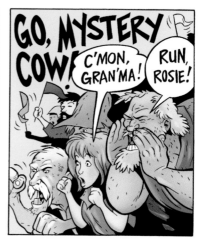

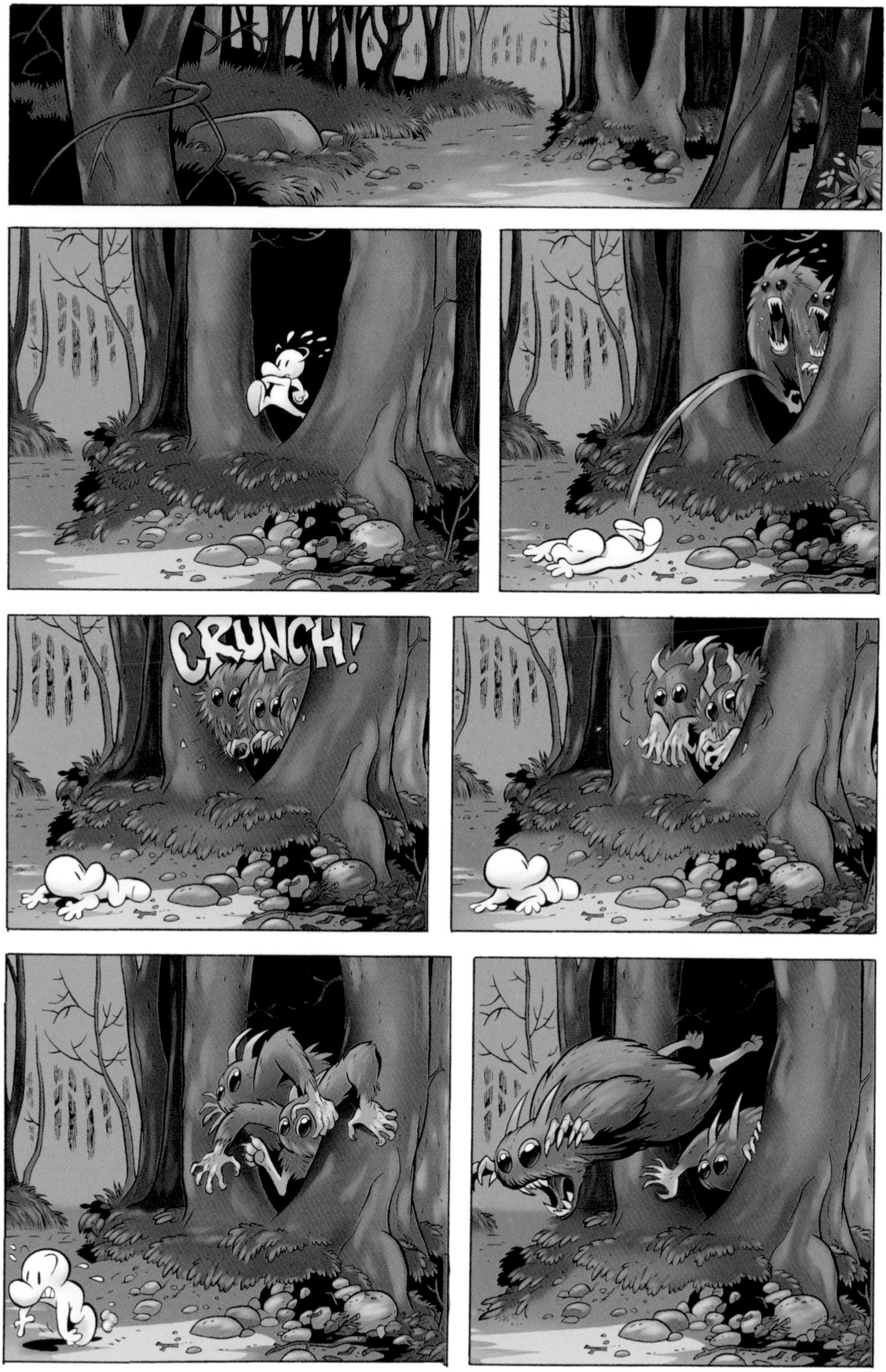
CRUNCH!

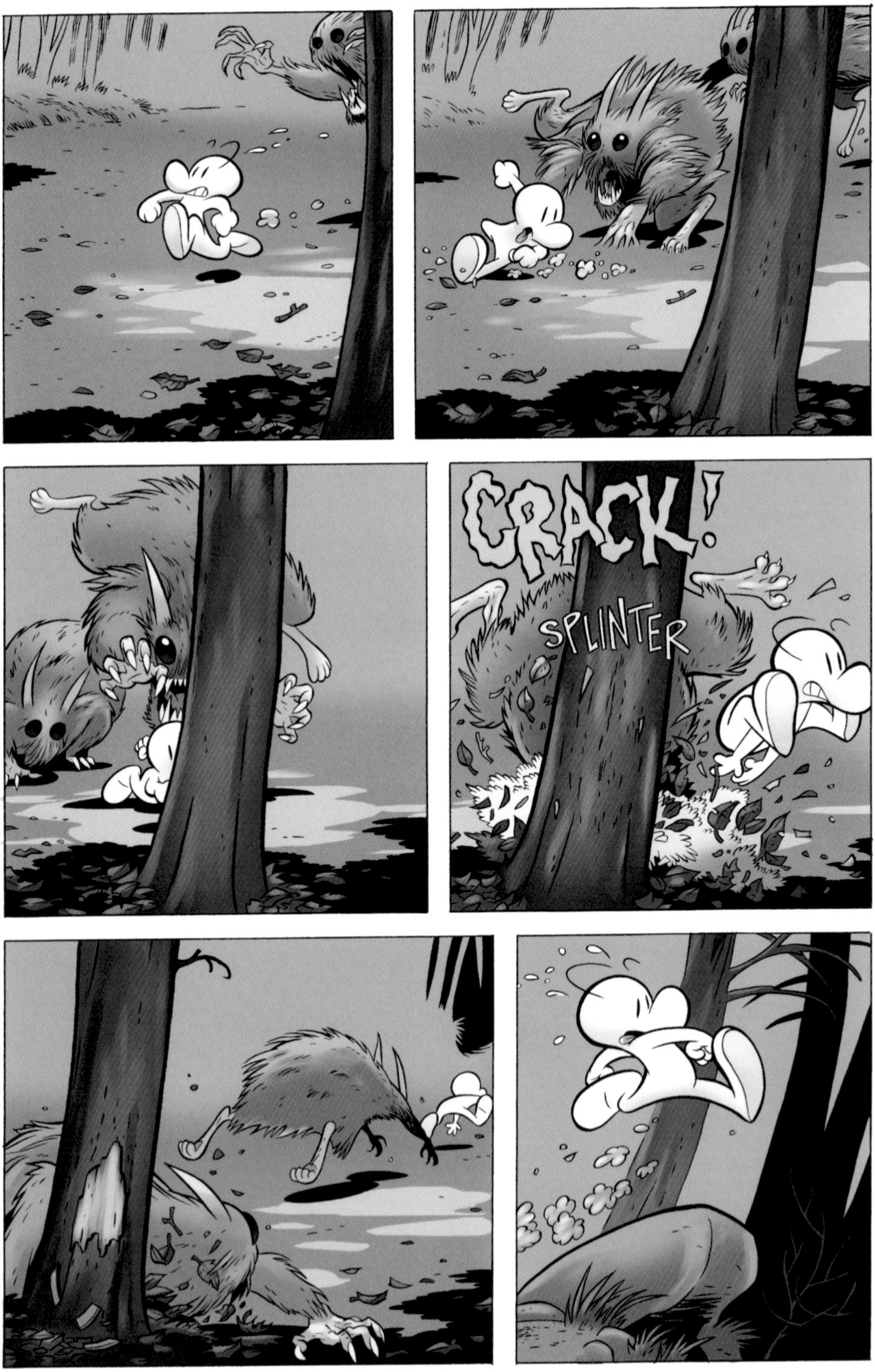
CRACK!
SPLINTER

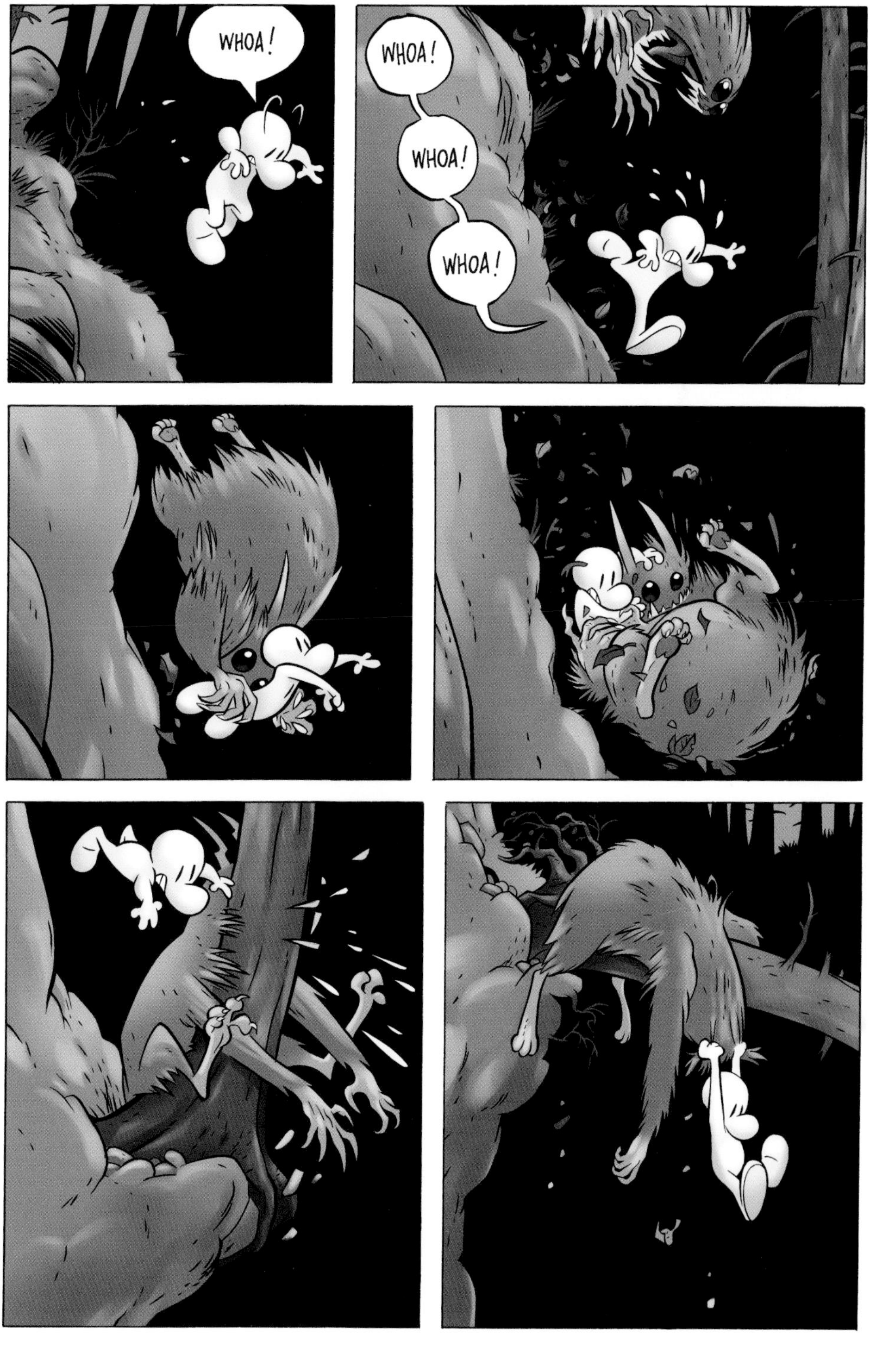
WHOA!
WHOA!
WHOA!
WHOA!

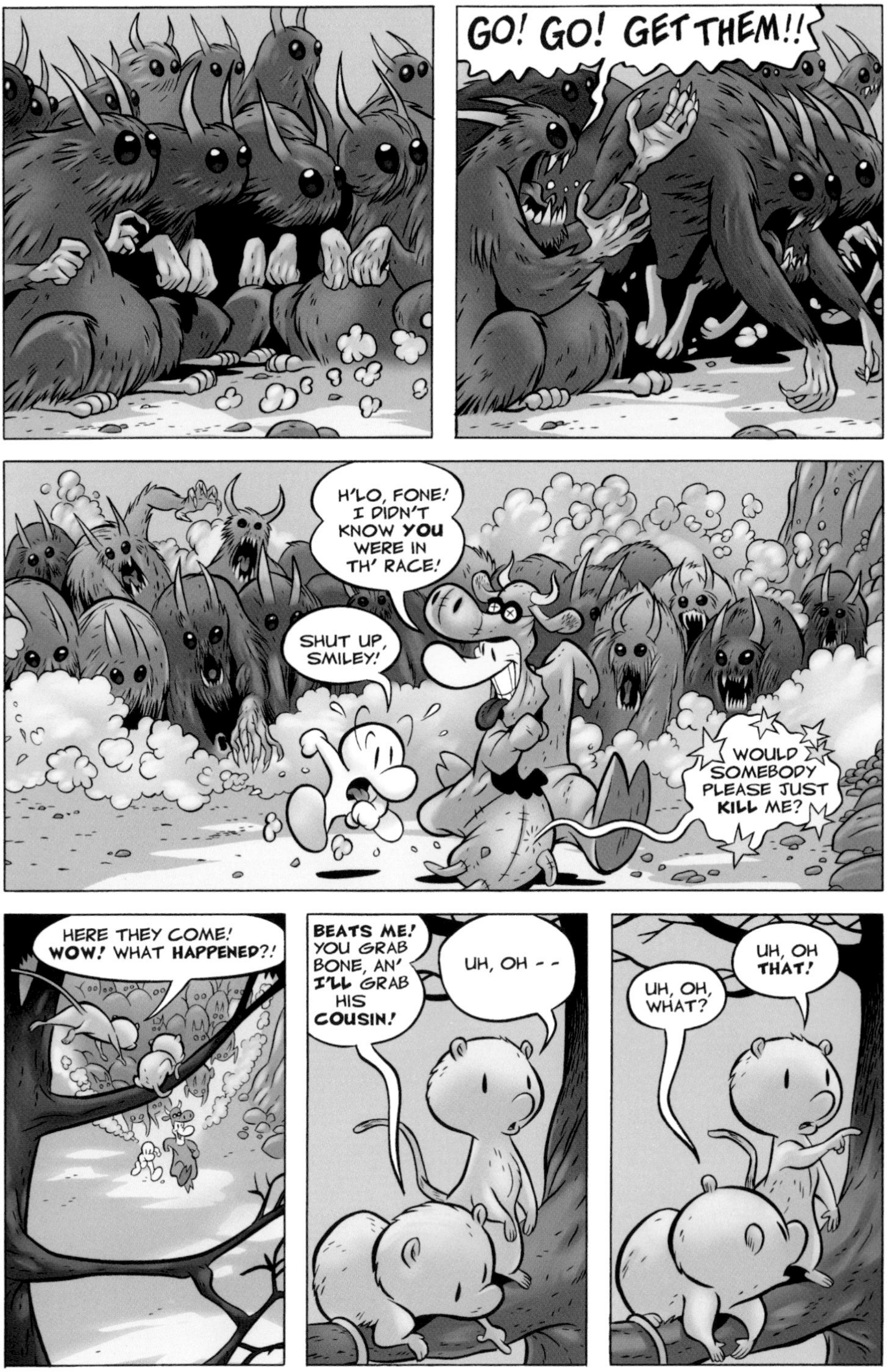
GO! GO! GET THEM!!
H'LO, FONE! I DIDN'T KNOW YOU WERE IN TH' RACE!
SHUT UP, SMILEY!
WOULD SOMEBODY PLEASE JUST KILL ME?
HERE THEY COME! WOW! WHAT HAPPENED?!
BEATS ME! YOU GRAB BONE, AN' I'LL GRAB HIS COUSIN!
UH, OH - -
UH, OH, WHAT?
UH, OH THAT!

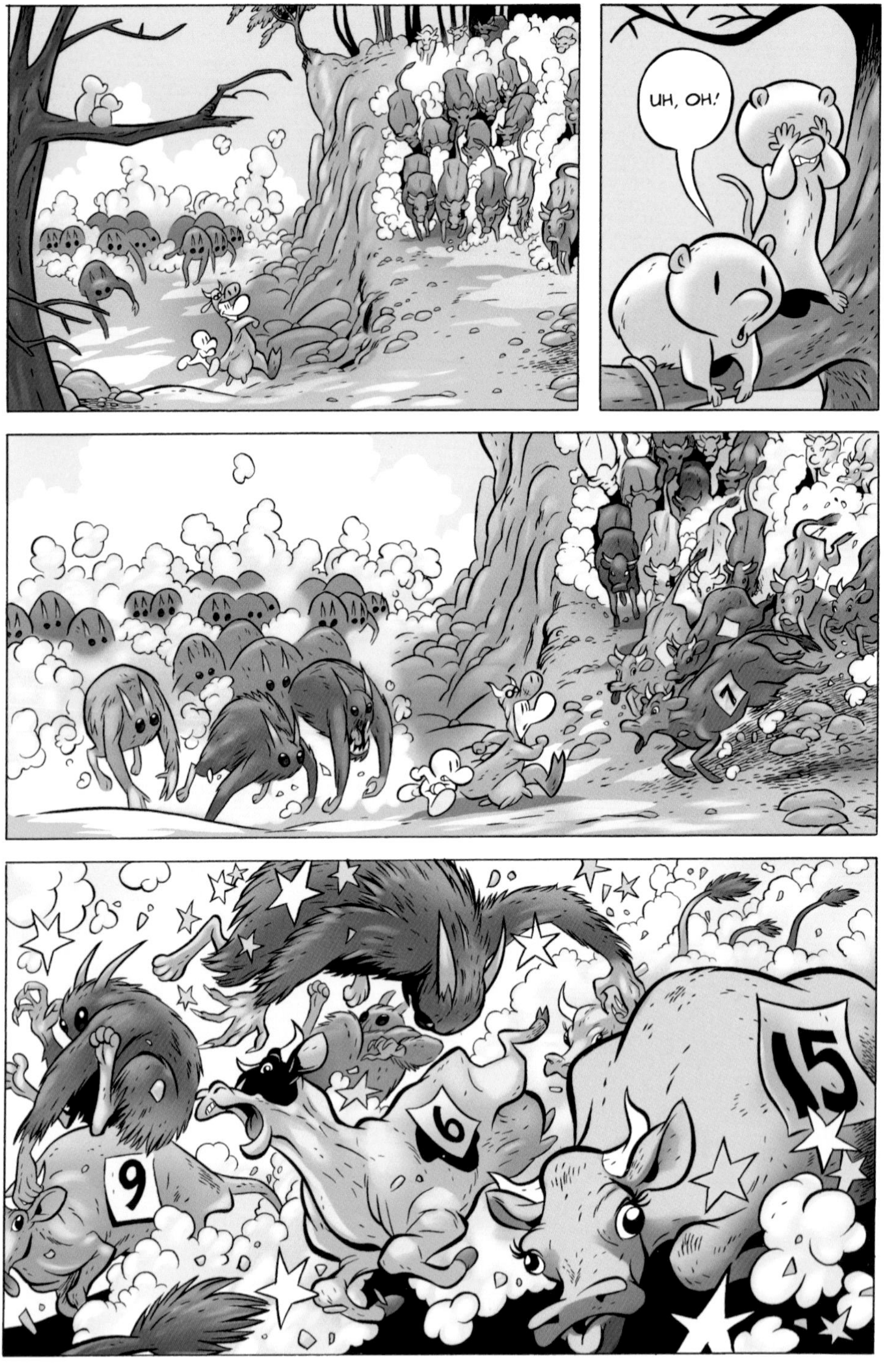
UH, OH!
7
15
6
9

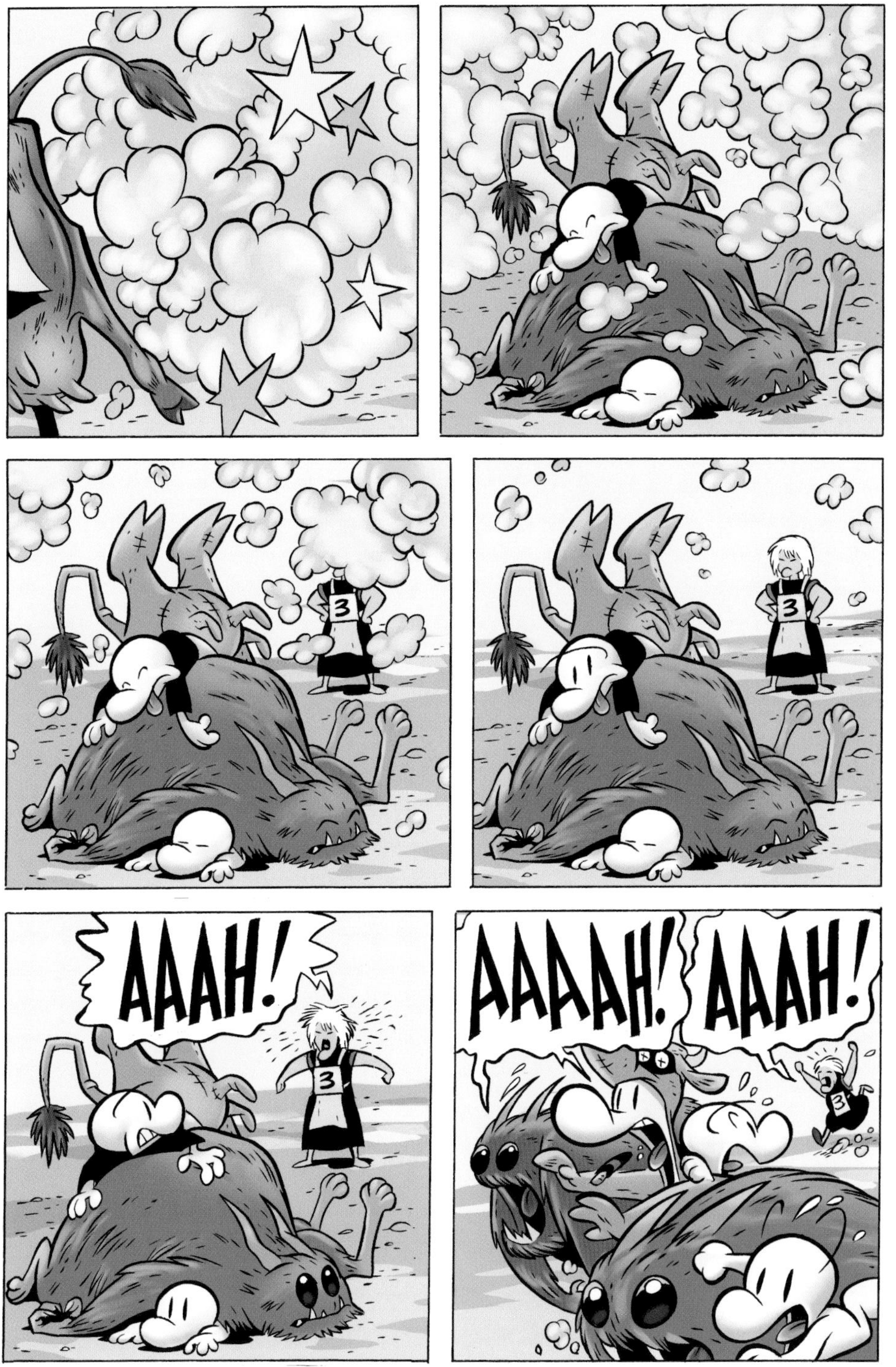
AAAH!
AAAAH!
AAAH!

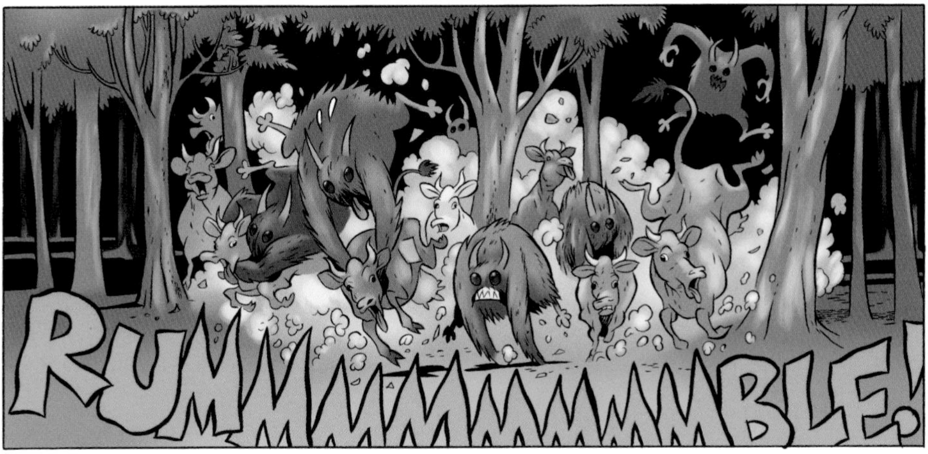
RUMMMMMMMMMMBLE!

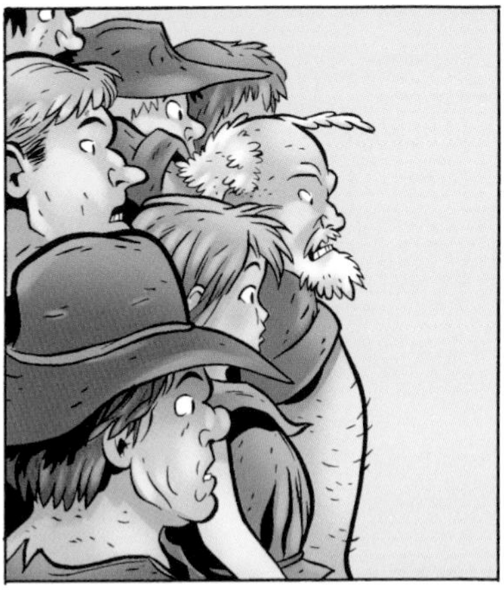

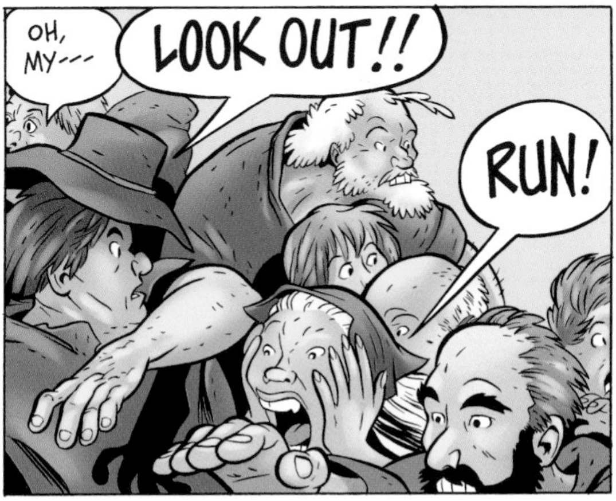
OH, MY---
LOOK OUT!!
RUN!

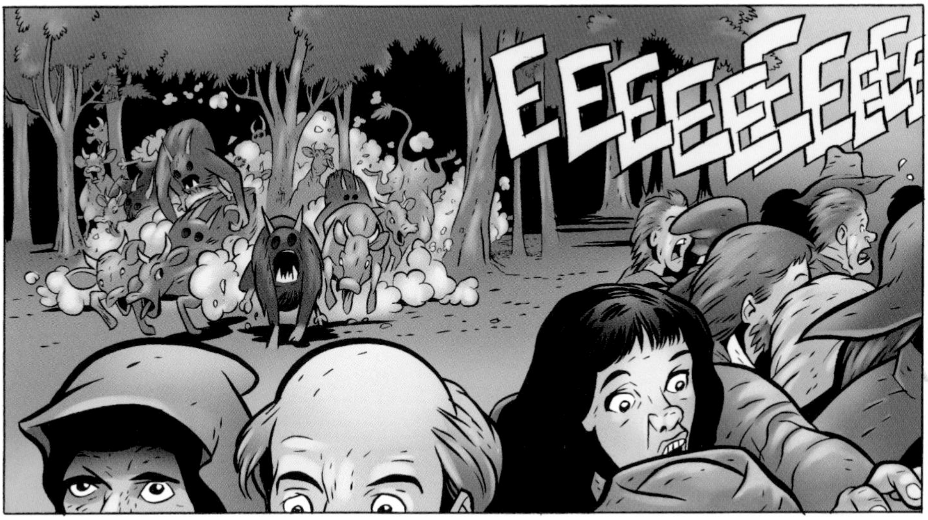
EEEEEEEEE

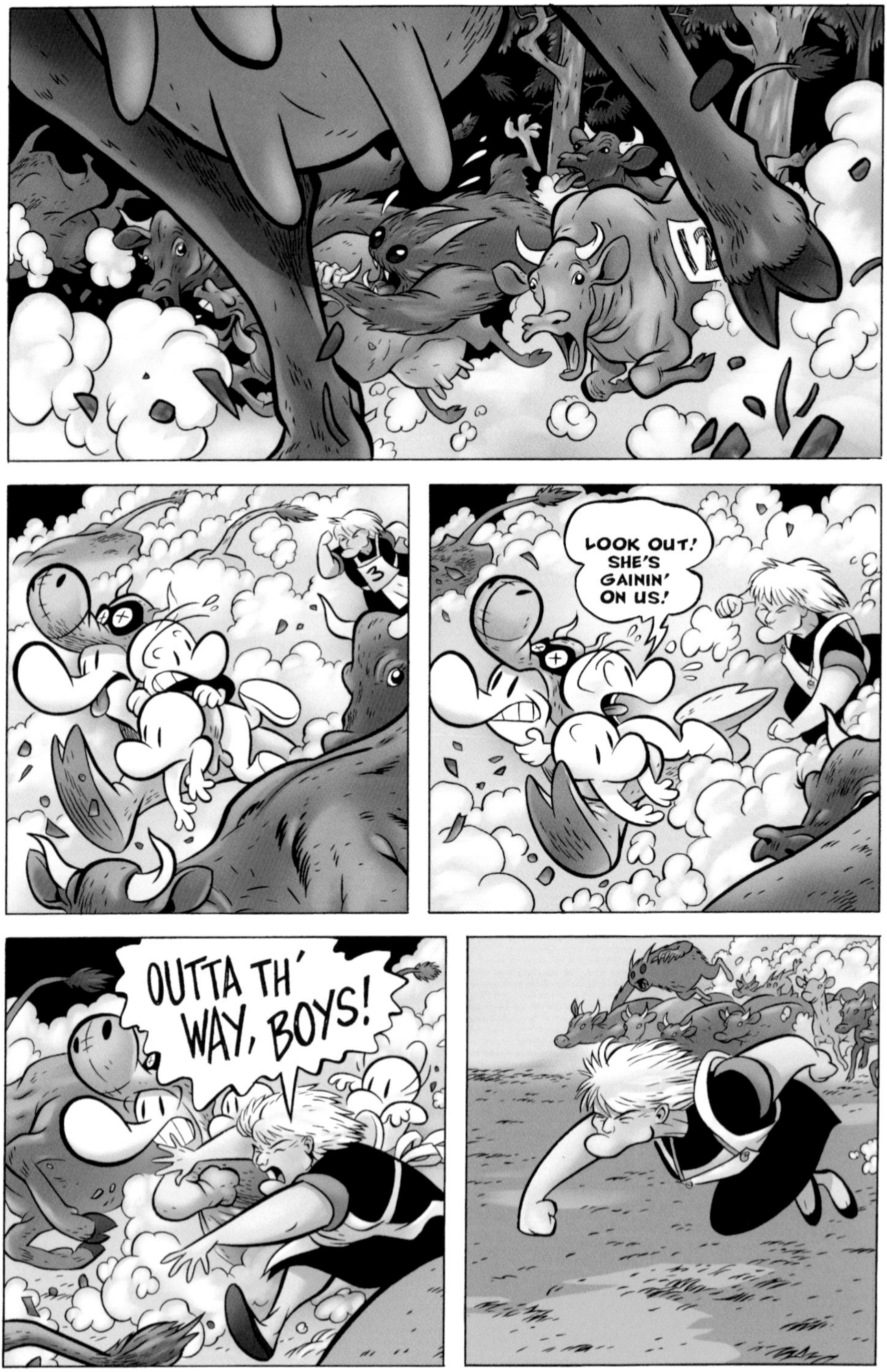
12
3
LOOK OUT! SHE'S GAININ' ON US!
OUTTA TH' WAY, BOYS!

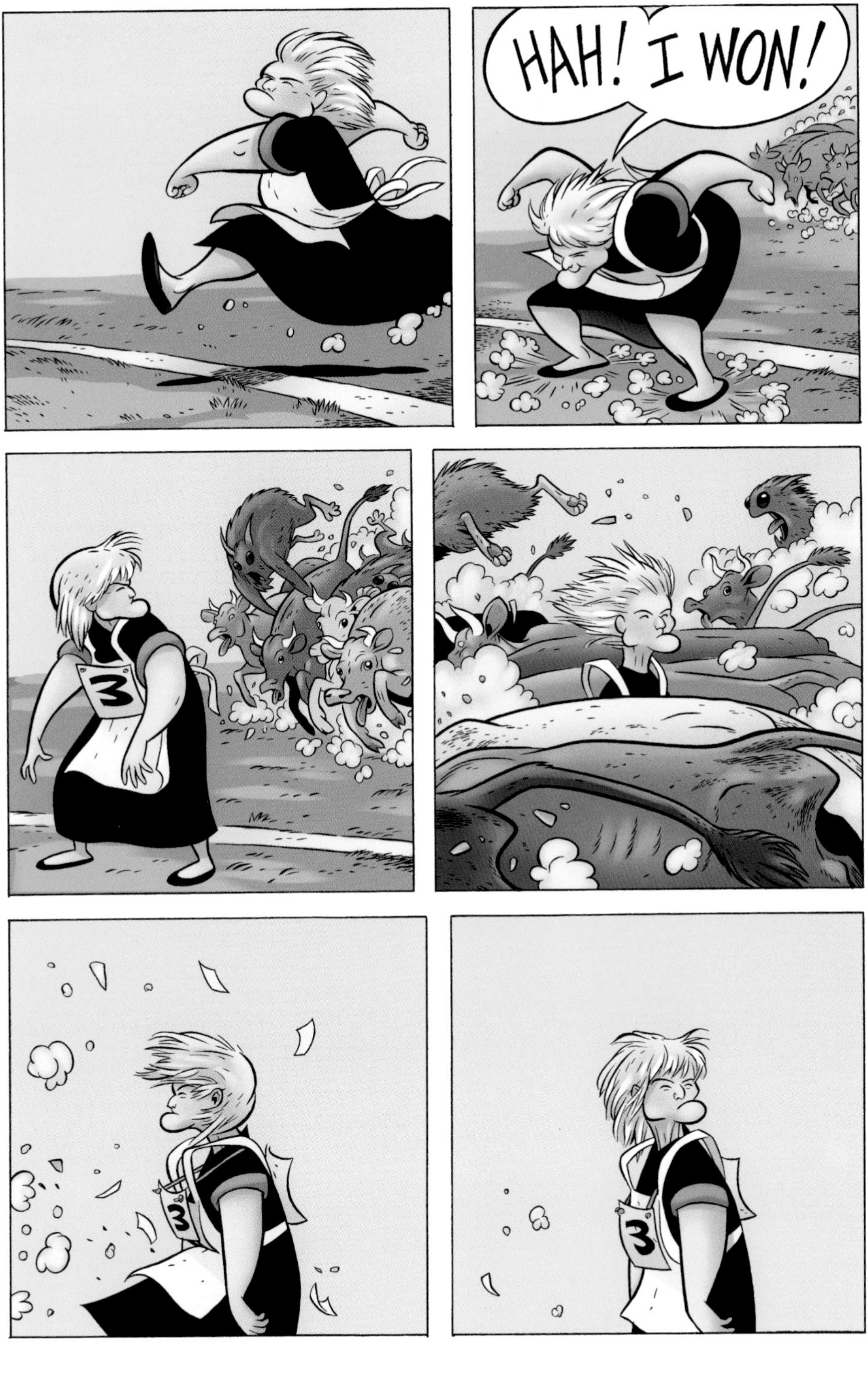
HAH! I WON!

I SAY WE LEAVE HIM THAT WAY.

GET HIM DOWN, THORN!

JUST A MOMENT... THERE!

IT'S ABOUT TIME!! GET ME DOWN FROM HERE!! THIS IS AN OUTRAGE! MY HANDS ARE GOIN' TO SLEEP!

I TOLD YOU TO LEAVE HIM!

PHONCIBLE P. BONE! YOU SHOULD BE GRATEFUL WE GOT YOU AWAY FROM THAT ANGRY MOB AT ALL! WHY, IF GRAN'MA HADN'T PROMISED TO COVER YOUR DEBTS FROM THE COW RACE, THINGS MIGHT'VE BEEN A LOT WORSE THAN BEING TIED TO A STAKE AND HIT WITH EGGS!

THAT MOB WAS OUT FOR BLOOD! WE BARELY HAD TIME TO THROW YOU IN TH' CART BEFORE THEY CHANGED THEIR MINDS!

OUT FOR BLOOD? SOUNDS TO ME LIKE THEY WERE OUT FOR STAKE 'N' EGGS!

SHUT UP, SMILEY!

HOW COME THEY DIDN'T TIE SMILEY TO A STAKE? HE WAS TH' ONE IN TH' COW SUIT!

AN' A STRIKING FIGURE OF A COW I MADE AT THAT!

YER BOTH IN TROUBLE!

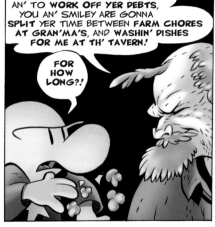

AN' TO WORK OFF YER DEBTS, YOU AN' SMILEY ARE GONNA SPLIT YER TIME BETWEEN FARM CHORES AT GRAN'MA'S, AND WASHIN' DISHES FOR ME AT TH' TAVERN!

FOR HOW LONG?!

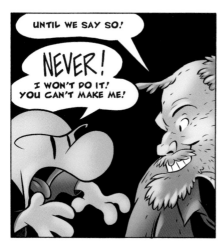

UNTIL WE SAY SO!

NEVER! I WON'T DO IT! YOU CAN'T MAKE ME!

TH' WAY I SEE IT, YOU BOYS ARE LUCKY TO BE ALIVE!

GRK!

KEEP YOUR VOICES DOWN! WE GOT AWAY FROM TH' VILLAGERS, BUT WE GOT WORSE TROUBLES NOW! THESE WOODS ARE DANGEROUS AT NIGHT!

I WONDER WHAT HAPPENED TO ALL THE RAT CREATURES AFTER THE RACE?

THEY DISAPPEARED INTO TH' FOREST.

FOR ALL WE KNOW, THEY MIGHT BE WATCHING US RIGHT NOW!

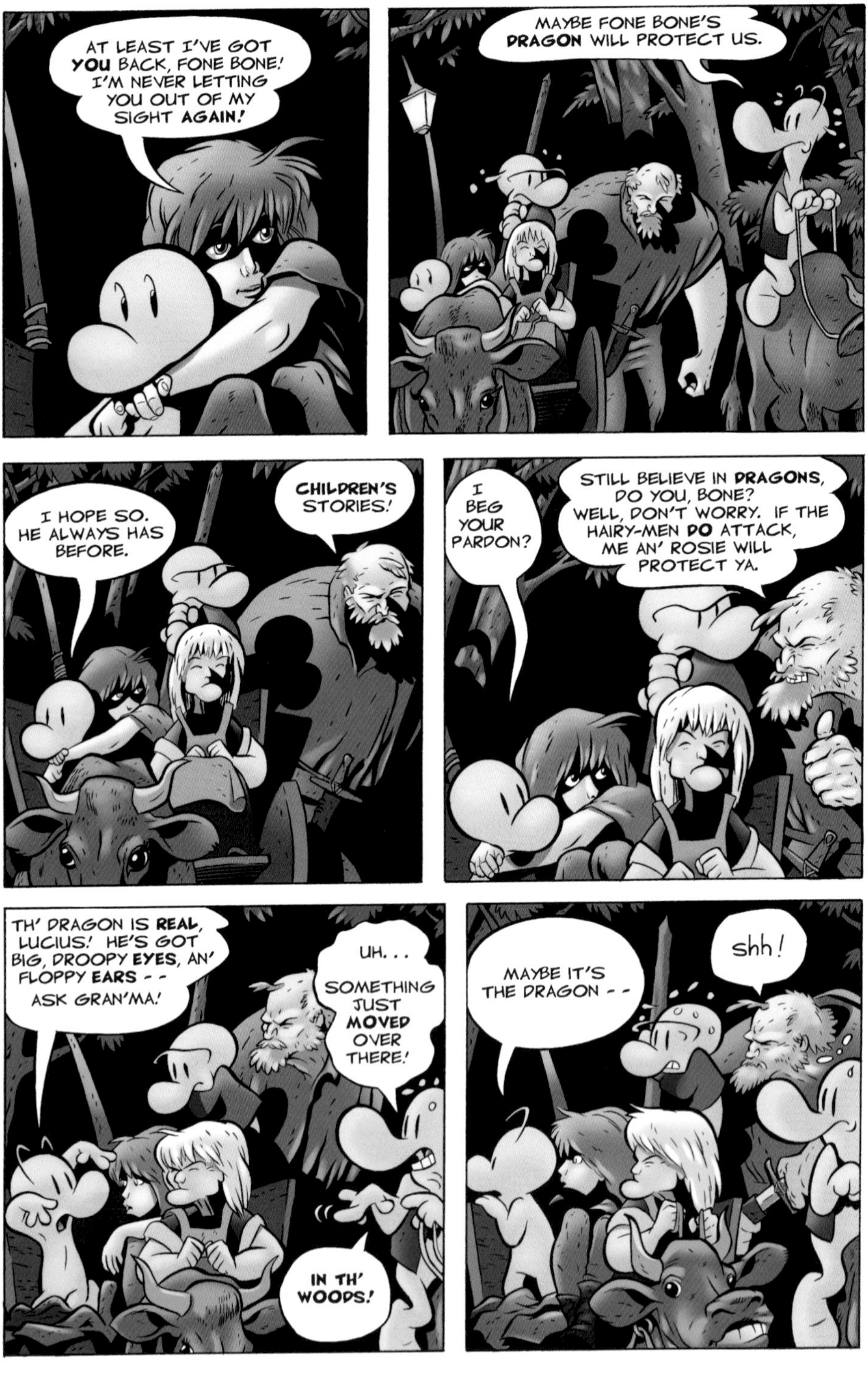
AT LEAST I'VE GOT YOU BACK, FONE BONE! I'M NEVER LETTING YOU OUT OF MY SIGHT AGAIN!
MAYBE FONE BONE'S DRAGON WILL PROTECT US.
I HOPE SO. HE ALWAYS HAS BEFORE.
CHILDREN'S STORIES!
I BEG YOUR PARDON?
STILL BELIEVE IN DRAGONS, DO YOU, BONE? WELL, DON'T WORRY. IF THE HAIRY-MEN DO ATTACK, ME AN' ROSIE WILL PROTECT YA.
TH' DRAGON IS REAL, LUCIUS! HE'S GOT BIG, DROOPY EYES, AN' FLOPPY EARS - - ASK GRAN'MA!
UH. . .
SOMETHING JUST MOVED OVER THERE!
IN TH' WOODS!
MAYBE IT'S THE DRAGON - -
shh!

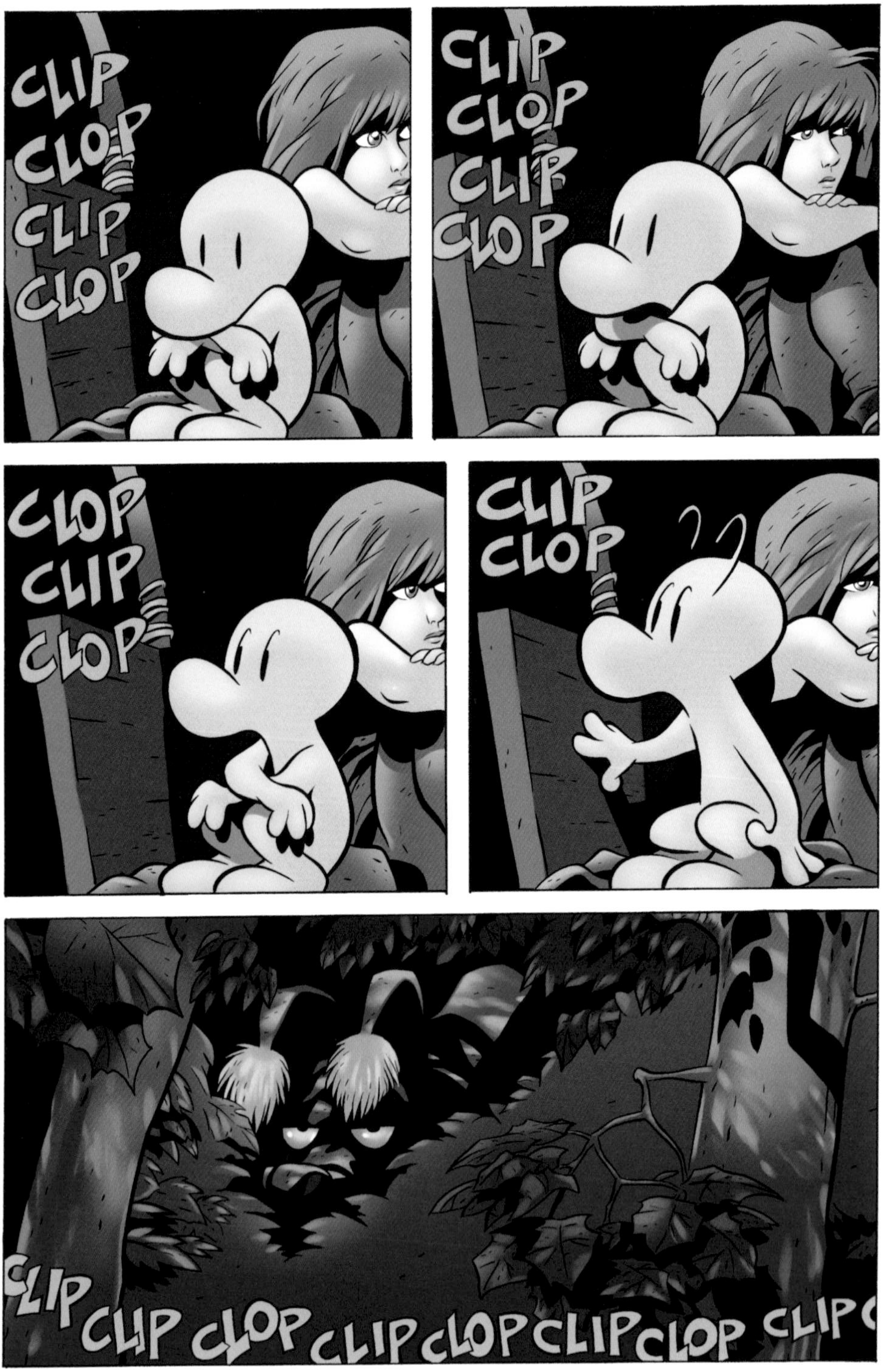
CLIP
CLOP
CLIP
CLOP
CLIP
CLOP
CLIP
CLOP
CLOP
CLIP
CLOP
CLIP
CLOP
CLIP CLIP CLOP CLIP CLOP CLIP CLOP CLIP

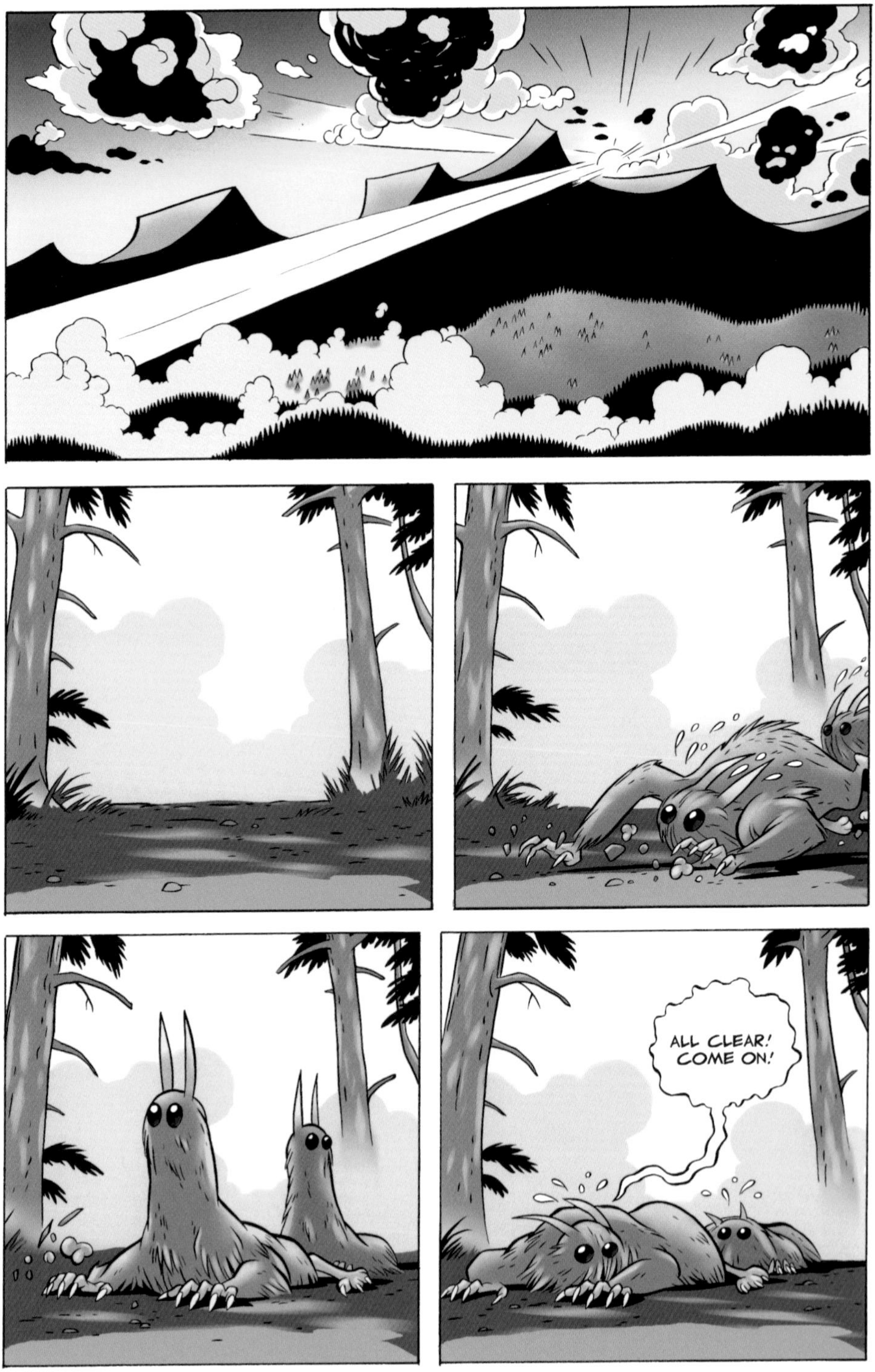
ALL CLEAR! COME ON!

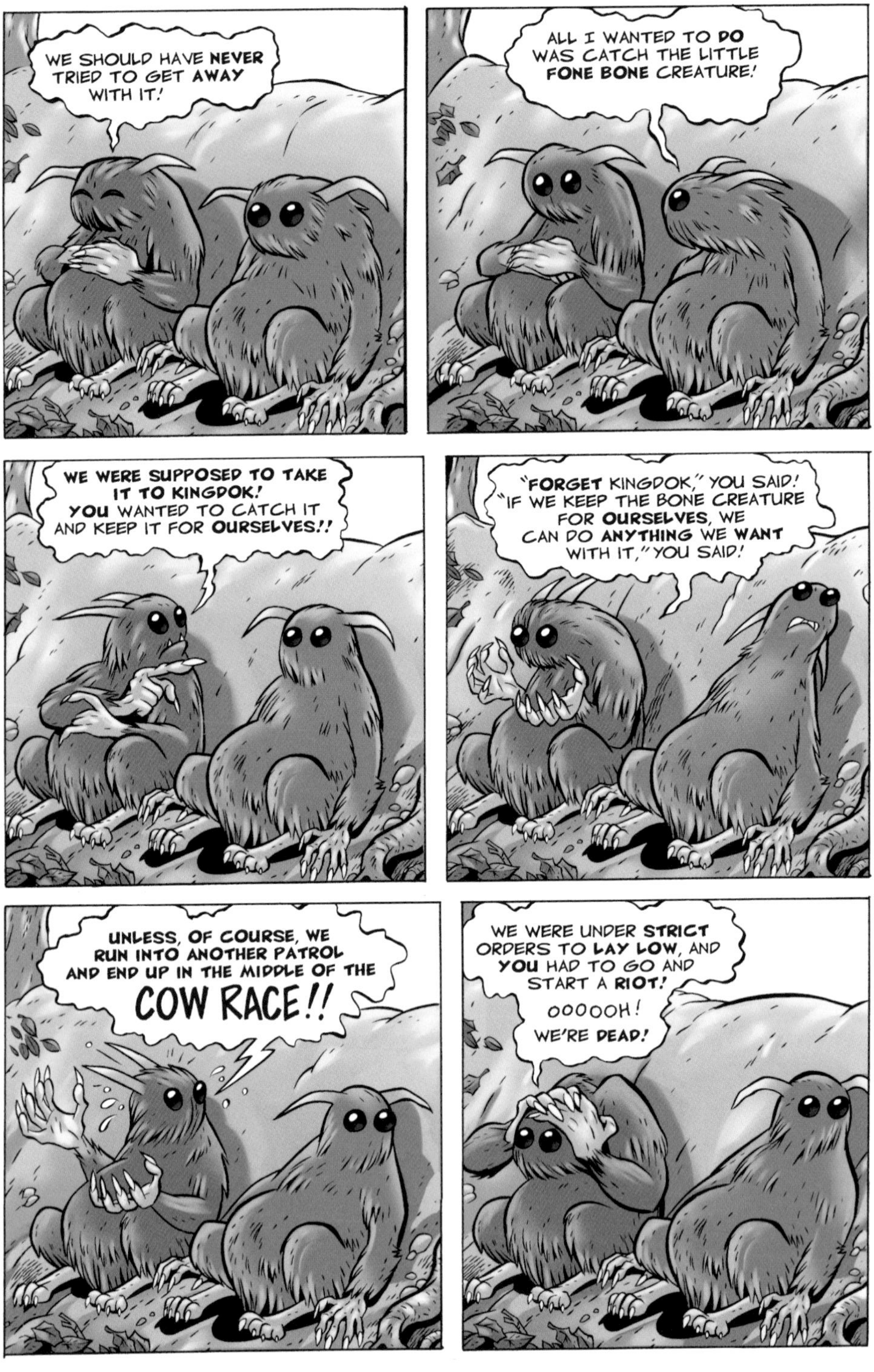
WE SHOULD HAVE NEVER TRIED TO GET AWAY WITH IT!
ALL I WANTED TO DO WAS CATCH THE LITTLE FONE BONE CREATURE!
WE WERE SUPPOSED TO TAKE IT TO KINGDOK! YOU WANTED TO CATCH IT AND KEEP IT FOR OURSELVES!!
"FORGET KINGDOK," YOU SAID! "IF WE KEEP THE BONE CREATURE FOR OURSELVES, WE CAN DO ANYTHING WE WANT WITH IT," YOU SAID!
UNLESS, OF COURSE, WE RUN INTO ANOTHER PATROL AND END UP IN THE MIDDLE OF THE COW RACE!!
WE WERE UNDER STRICT ORDERS TO LAY LOW, AND YOU HAD TO GO AND START A RIOT!
OOOOOH!
WE'RE DEAD!

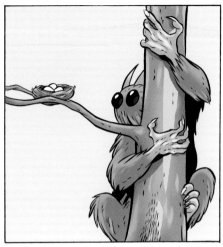

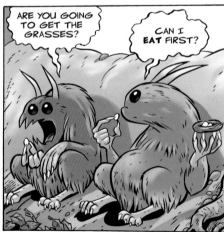

WELL... THE **BEAMS** ARE SOUND. MOST OF TH' **DAMAGE** IS TO TH' **ROOF.**

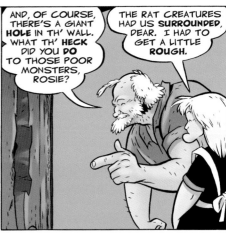

AND, OF COURSE, THERE'S A GIANT **HOLE** IN TH' WALL. WHAT TH' **HECK** DID YOU **DO** TO THOSE POOR MONSTERS, ROSIE?

THE RAT CREATURES HAD US **SURROUNDED**, DEAR. I HAD TO GET A LITTLE **ROUGH.**

THIS PLACE LOOKS LIKE A **BATTLEFIELD!** YOU'RE LUCKY YOU ESCAPED WITH YOUR **LIVES!**

IT **WAS** A BIT SCARY, BUT DON'T FORGET **I** FOUGHT TH' RATS BACK IN TH' BIG WAR!

ROSE, I'M **SERIOUS!** THIS WASN'T SOME BACKWOODS **RAID** ON **LIVESTOCK!** THIS WAS A FULL-FLEDGED **ATTACK!**

I KNOW THAT, DEAR. THAT'S WHY I ASKED YOU TO COME ALONG.

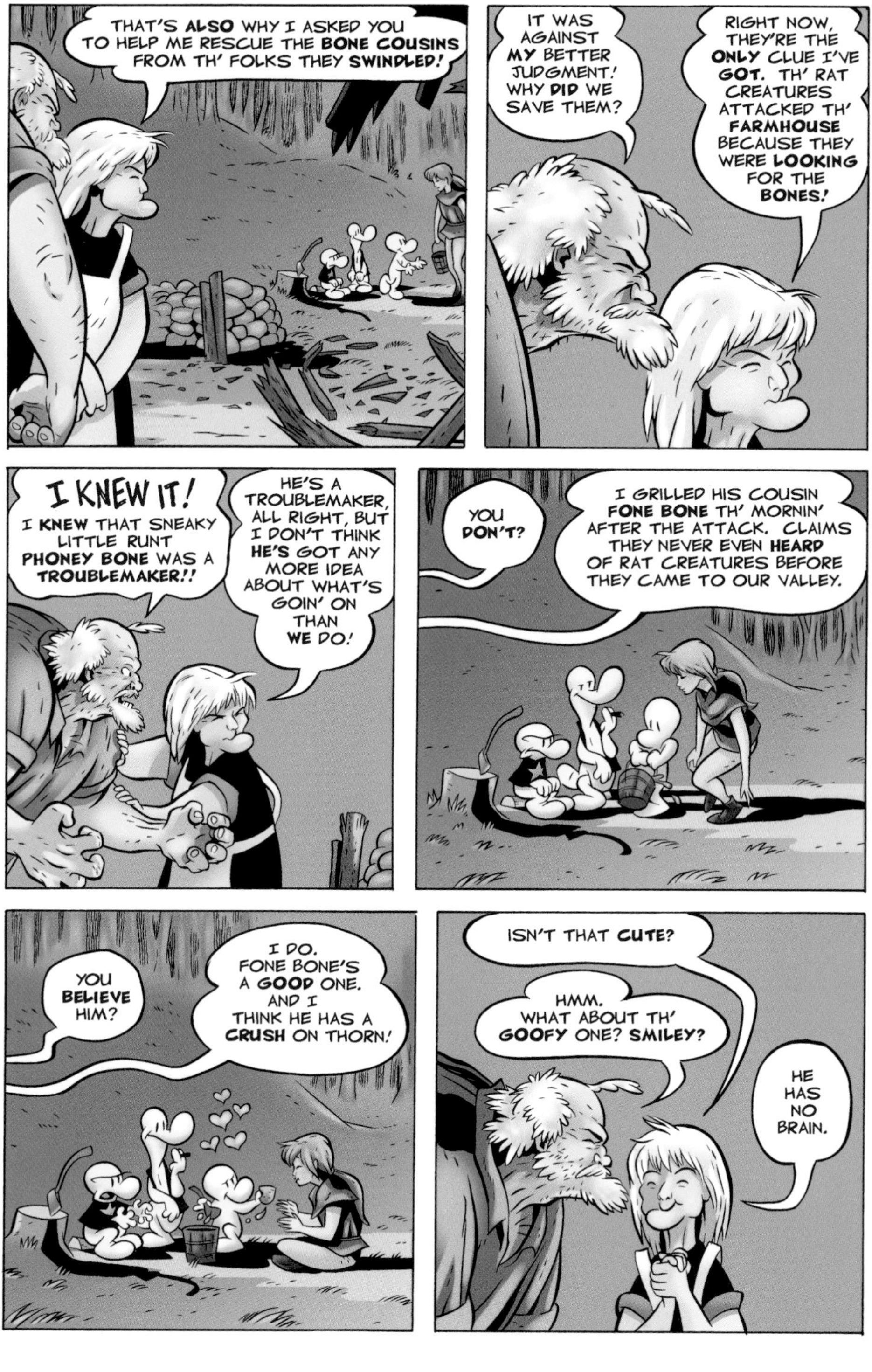
THAT'S ALSO WHY I ASKED YOU TO HELP ME RESCUE THE BONE COUSINS FROM TH' FOLKS THEY SWINDLED!
IT WAS AGAINST MY BETTER JUDGMENT! WHY DID WE SAVE THEM?
RIGHT NOW, THEY'RE THE ONLY CLUE I'VE GOT. TH' RAT CREATURES ATTACKED TH' FARMHOUSE BECAUSE THEY WERE LOOKING FOR THE BONES!
I KNEW IT! I KNEW THAT SNEAKY LITTLE RUNT PHONEY BONE WAS A TROUBLEMAKER!!
HE'S A TROUBLEMAKER, ALL RIGHT, BUT I DON'T THINK HE'S GOT ANY MORE IDEA ABOUT WHAT'S GOIN' ON THAN WE DO!
YOU DON'T?
I GRILLED HIS COUSIN FONE BONE TH' MORNIN' AFTER THE ATTACK. CLAIMS THEY NEVER EVEN HEARD OF RAT CREATURES BEFORE THEY CAME TO OUR VALLEY.
YOU BELIEVE HIM?
I DO. FONE BONE'S A GOOD ONE. AND I THINK HE HAS A CRUSH ON THORN!
ISN'T THAT CUTE?
HMM. WHAT ABOUT TH' GOOFY ONE? SMILEY?
HE HAS NO BRAIN.

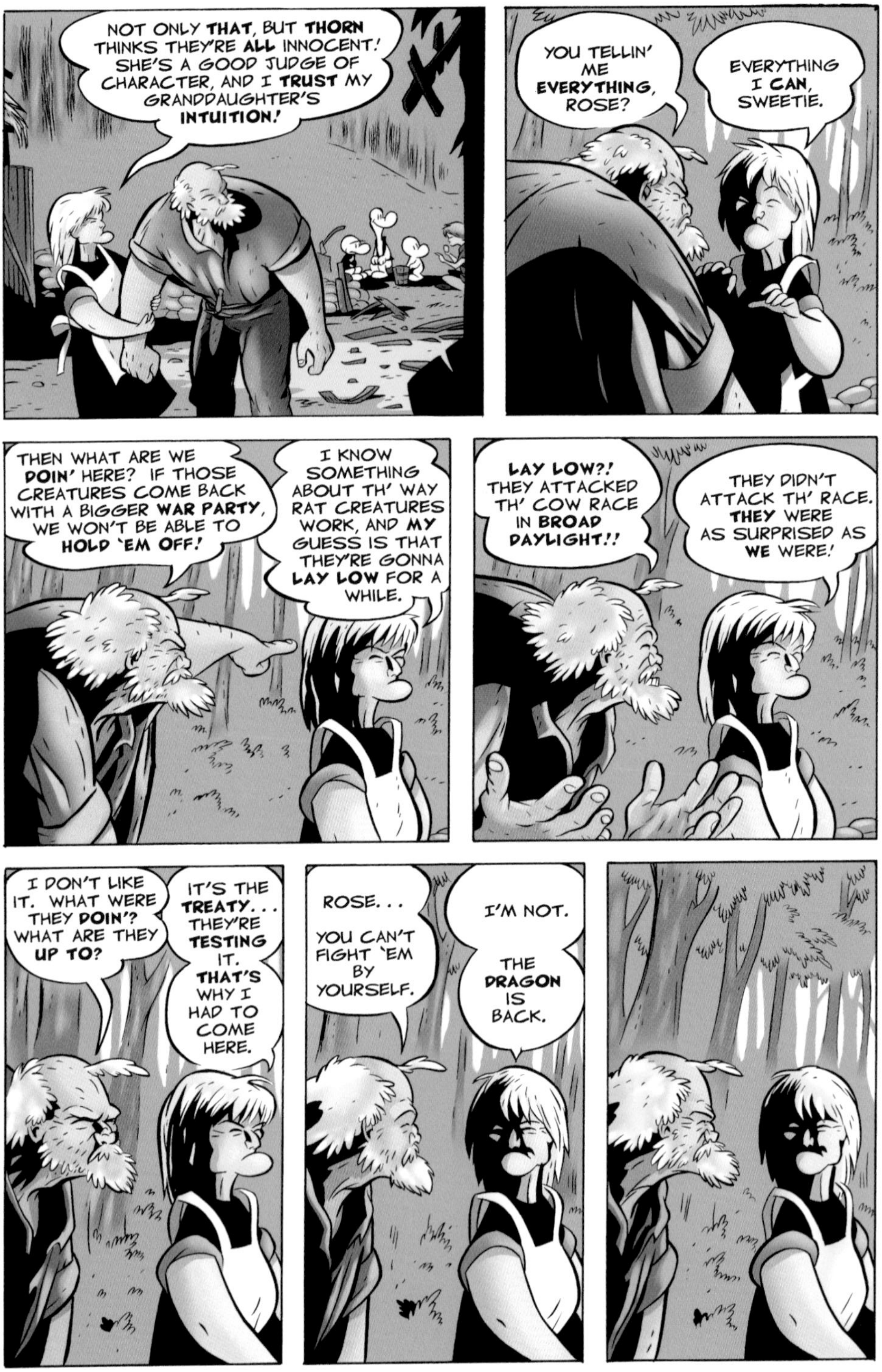
NOT ONLY THAT, BUT THORN THINKS THEY'RE ALL INNOCENT! SHE'S A GOOD JUDGE OF CHARACTER, AND I TRUST MY GRANDDAUGHTER'S INTUITION!
YOU TELLIN' ME EVERYTHING, ROSE?
EVERYTHING I CAN, SWEETIE.
THEN WHAT ARE WE DOIN' HERE? IF THOSE CREATURES COME BACK WITH A BIGGER WAR PARTY, WE WON'T BE ABLE TO HOLD 'EM OFF!
I KNOW SOMETHING ABOUT TH' WAY RAT CREATURES WORK, AND MY GUESS IS THAT THEY'RE GONNA LAY LOW FOR A WHILE.
LAY LOW?! THEY ATTACKED TH' COW RACE IN BROAD DAYLIGHT!!
THEY DIDN'T ATTACK TH' RACE. THEY WERE AS SURPRISED AS WE WERE!
I DON'T LIKE IT. WHAT WERE THEY DOIN'? WHAT ARE THEY UP TO?
IT'S THE TREATY... THEY'RE TESTING IT. THAT'S WHY I HAD TO COME HERE.
ROSE...
YOU CAN'T FIGHT 'EM BY YOURSELF.
I'M NOT.
THE DRAGON IS BACK.

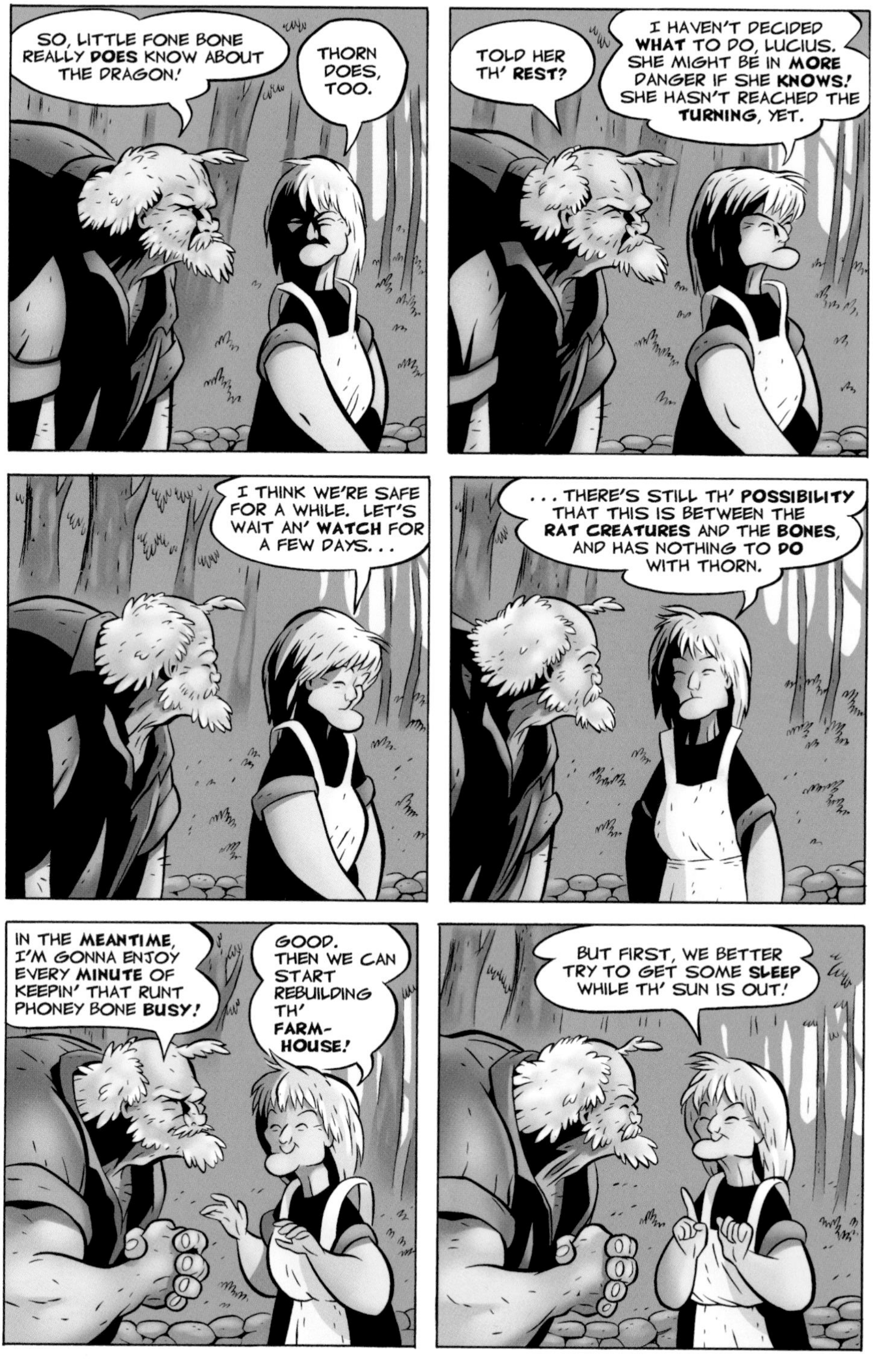
SO, LITTLE FONE BONE REALLY DOES KNOW ABOUT THE DRAGON!
THORN DOES, TOO.
TOLD HER TH' REST?
I HAVEN'T DECIDED WHAT TO DO, LUCIUS. SHE MIGHT BE IN MORE DANGER IF SHE KNOWS! SHE HASN'T REACHED THE TURNING, YET.
I THINK WE'RE SAFE FOR A WHILE. LET'S WAIT AN' WATCH FOR A FEW DAYS...
...THERE'S STILL TH' POSSIBILITY THAT THIS IS BETWEEN THE RAT CREATURES AND THE BONES, AND HAS NOTHING TO DO WITH THORN.
IN THE MEANTIME, I'M GONNA ENJOY EVERY MINUTE OF KEEPIN' THAT RUNT PHONEY BONE BUSY!
GOOD. THEN WE CAN START REBUILDING TH' FARM-HOUSE!
BUT FIRST, WE BETTER TRY TO GET SOME SLEEP WHILE TH' SUN IS OUT!

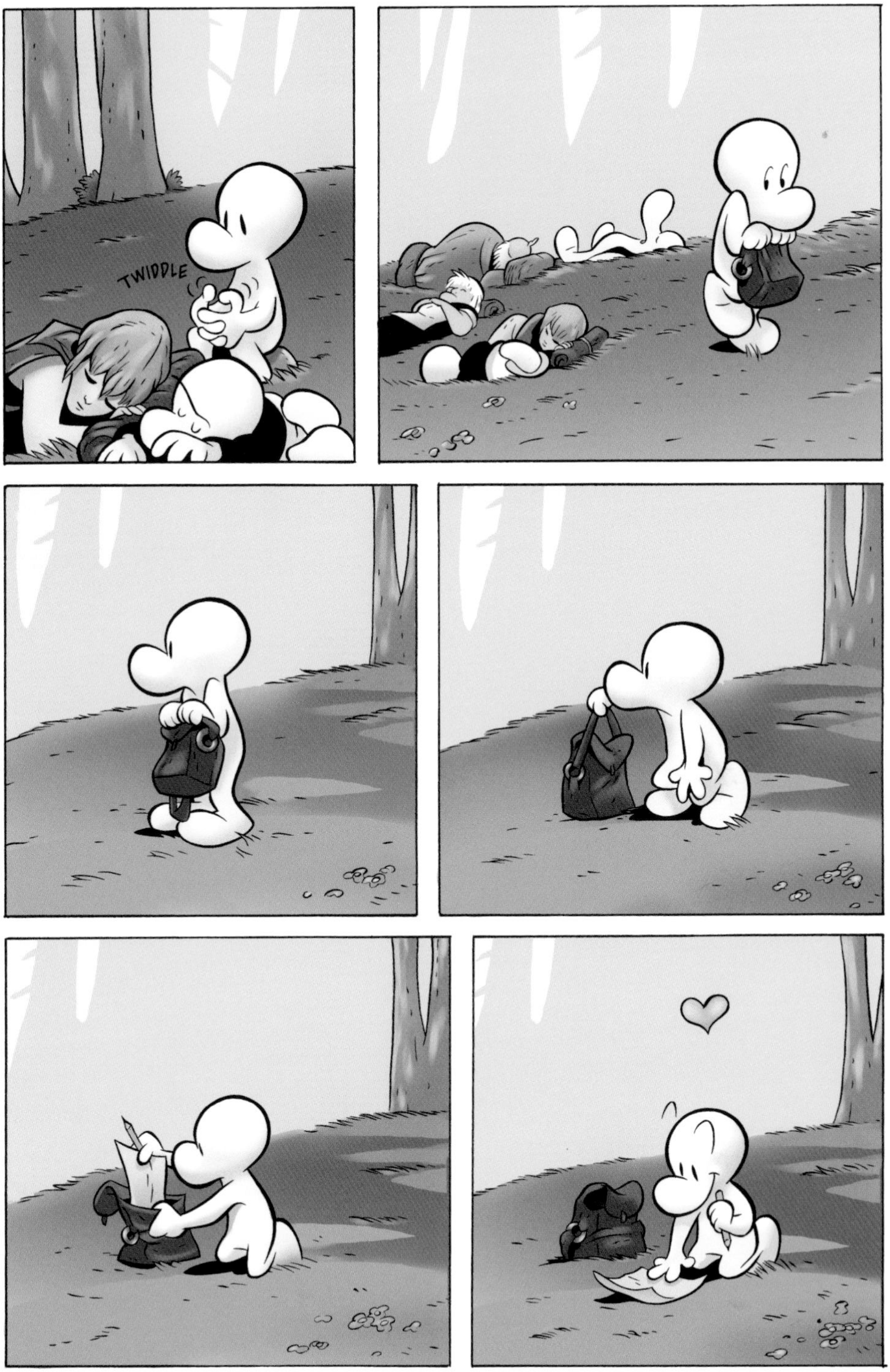
TWIDDLE

'ROUND AND 'ROUND
OUR BUSY FEET GO

HURRY AND FURY
AND APPLE-RED GLOW...

THE SIGHTS AND SOUNDS
OF PLACES TO DO...

THE LAUGHING AND SHOUTING WILL NEVER BE THROUGH!

But...

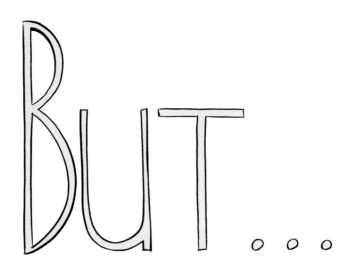

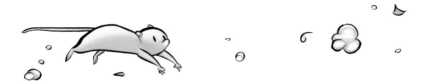

After all that running, the rest is best

AND THE BEST TO REST WITH
IS YOU.

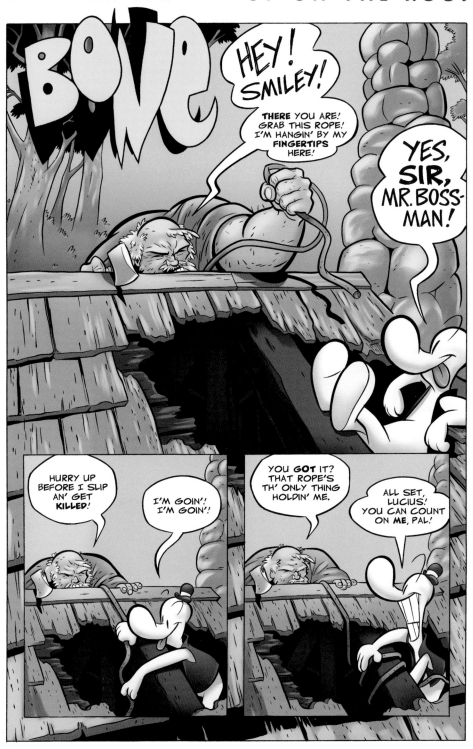

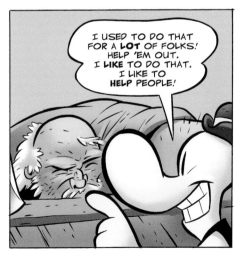

SMILEY.

THERE WAS THIS **GREAT** PLACE DOWN IN TH' PARK BY THE OL' STATUE OF **BIG JOHNSON BONE** WHERE YOU COULD SIT AN' FEED TH' **BIRDS.** . . .

SMILEY!

THAT WAS MY **REAL** JOB, Y'KNOW! CHASE AWAY TH' PIGEONS AN' GET THOSE LITTLE PIECES OF **BREAD.** . . .

HIII-YAH!

SMILEY! I'M NOT HANGIN' AROUND HERE FOR MY HEALTH! I'M TRYIN' TO FIX TH' ROOF!!

ANYTHING I CAN DO TO HELP?

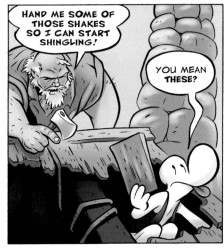

HAND ME SOME OF THOSE SHAKES SO I CAN START SHINGLING!

YOU MEAN **THESE**?

YES. GIMME ENOUGH FOR MY SIDE.

HOW MANY IS **THAT**? THERE'S A WHOLE **PILE** UNDER HERE.

WELL, IF **HALF** OF TH' PILE IS FOR **YOUR** SIDE OF TH' ROOF, AN' **HALF** IS FOR MY SIDE, **YOU FIGURE IT OUT!**

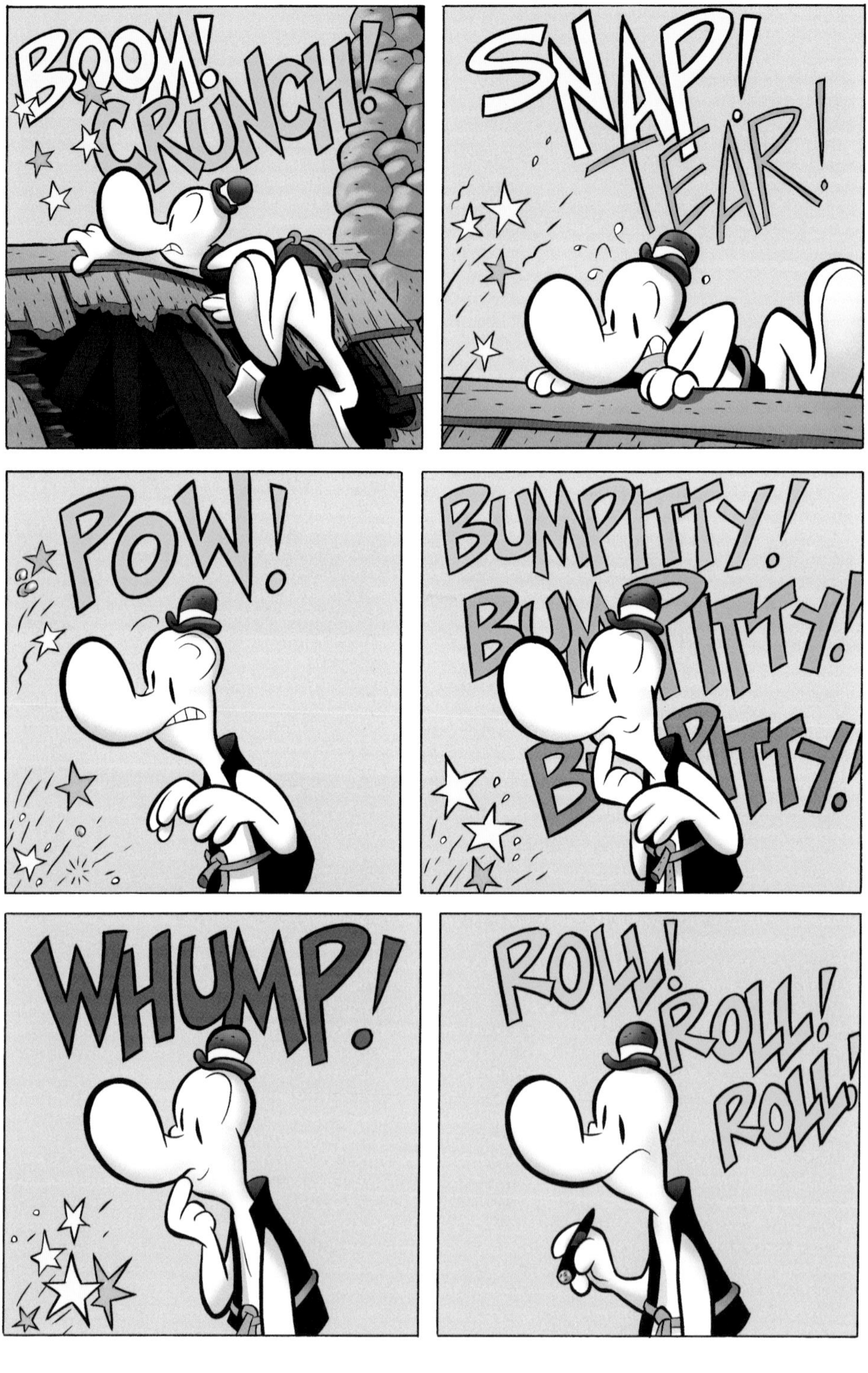
BOOM!
CRUNCH!
SNAP!
TEAR!
POW!
BUMPITTY!
BUMPITTY!
BUMPITTY!
WHUMP!
ROLL!
ROLL!
ROLL!

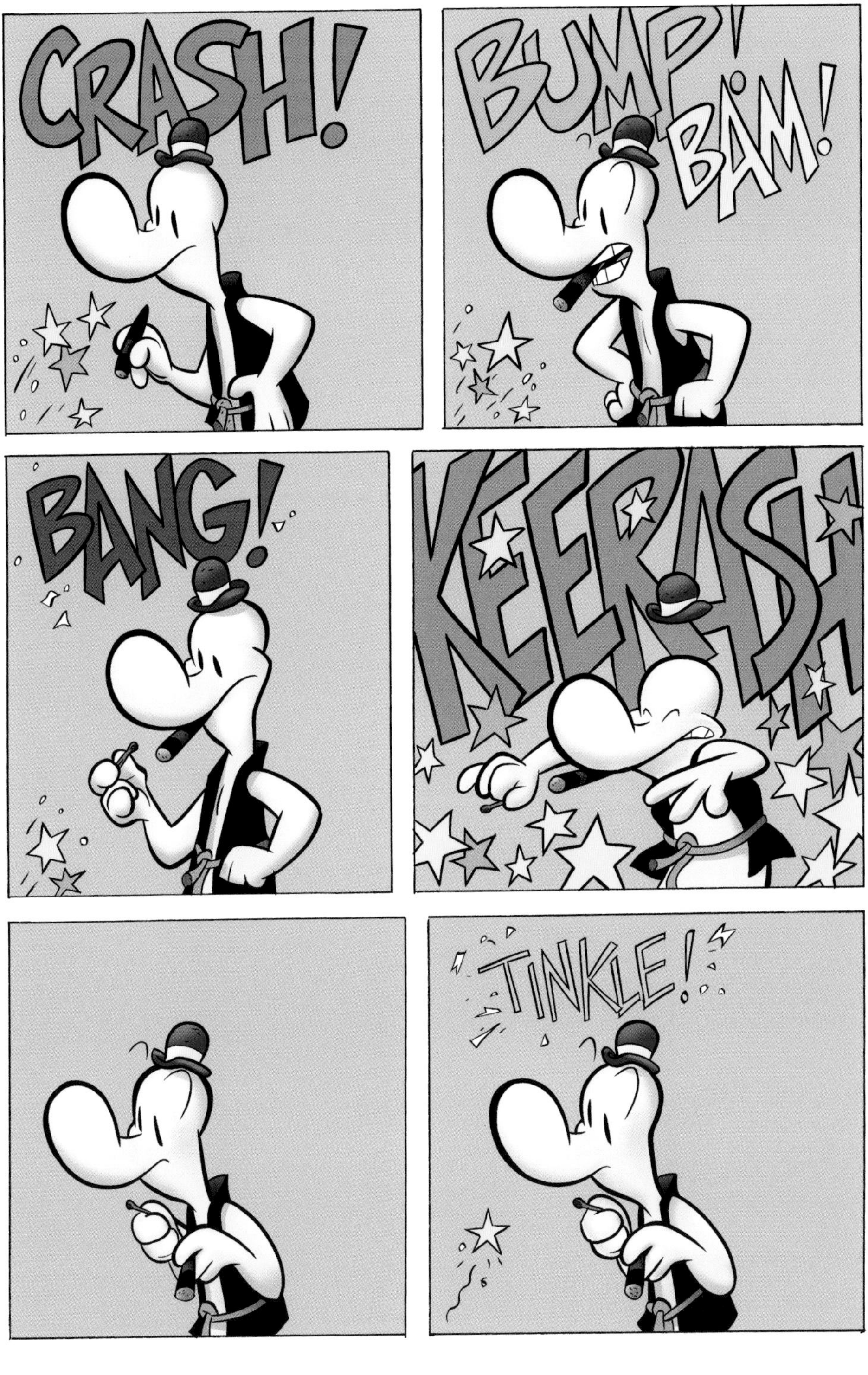
CRASH!
BUMP!
BAM!
BANG!
KEERASH
TINKLE!

...TO BE CONTINUED.

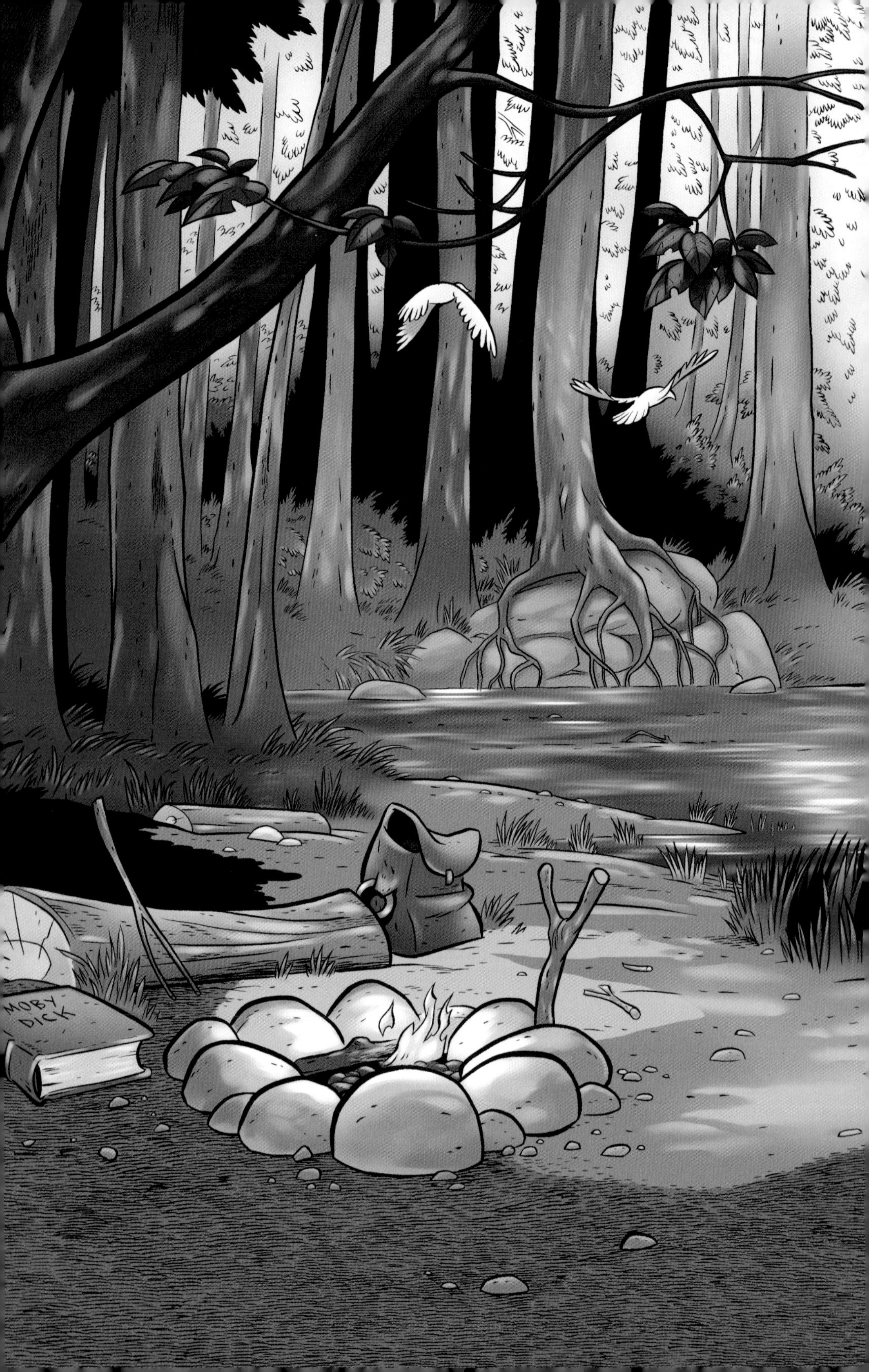
MOBY
DICK

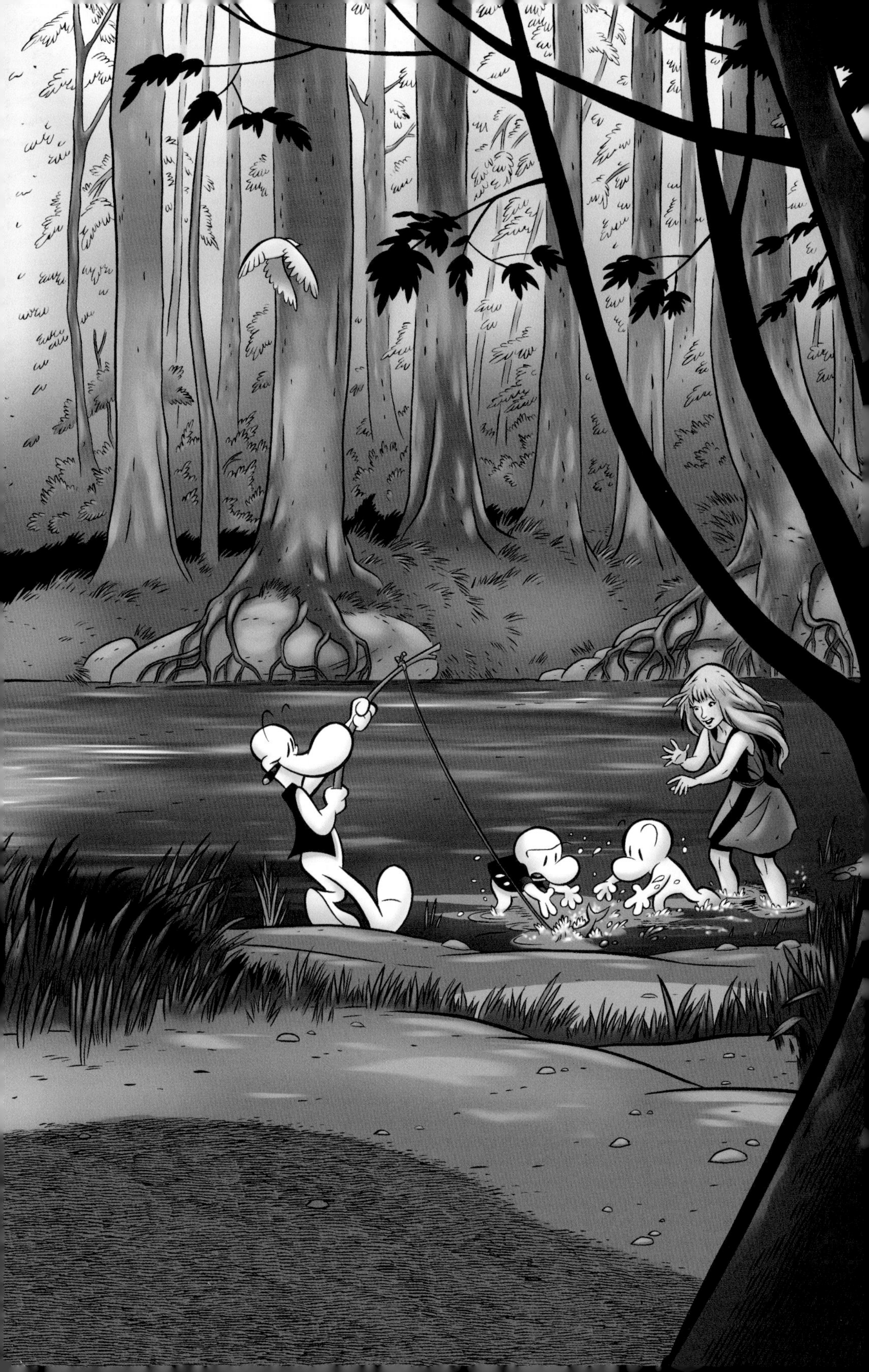

About JEFF SMITH

JEFF SMITH was born and raised in the American Midwest. He learned about cartooning from comic strips, comic books, and watching animated shorts on TV. After four years of drawing comic strips for Ohio State University's student newspaper and cofounding Character Builders animation studio in 1986, Smith launched the comic book *BONE* in 1991. Between *BONE* and other comics projects, Smith spends much of his time on the international guest circuit promoting comics and the art of graphic novels.

More about *BONE*

An instant classic when it first appeared in the U.S. as an underground comic book in 1991, *BONE* has since garnered 38 international awards and sold a million copies in 15 languages. Now, Scholastic's GRAPHIX imprint is publishing full-color graphic novel editions of the nine-book *BONE* series. Look for the continuing adventures of the Bone cousins in *Eyes of the Storm*.

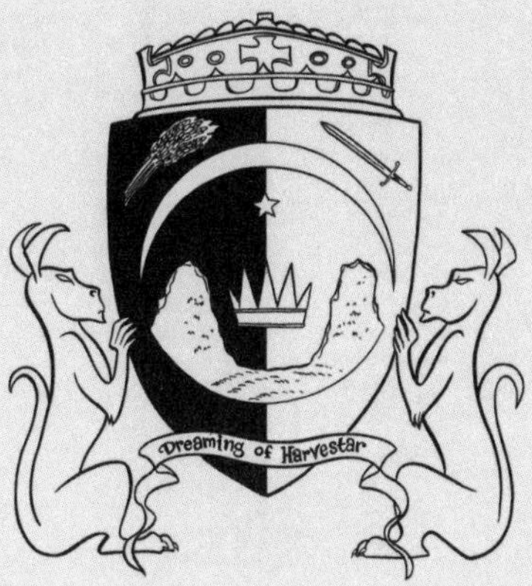
Dreaming of Harvestar

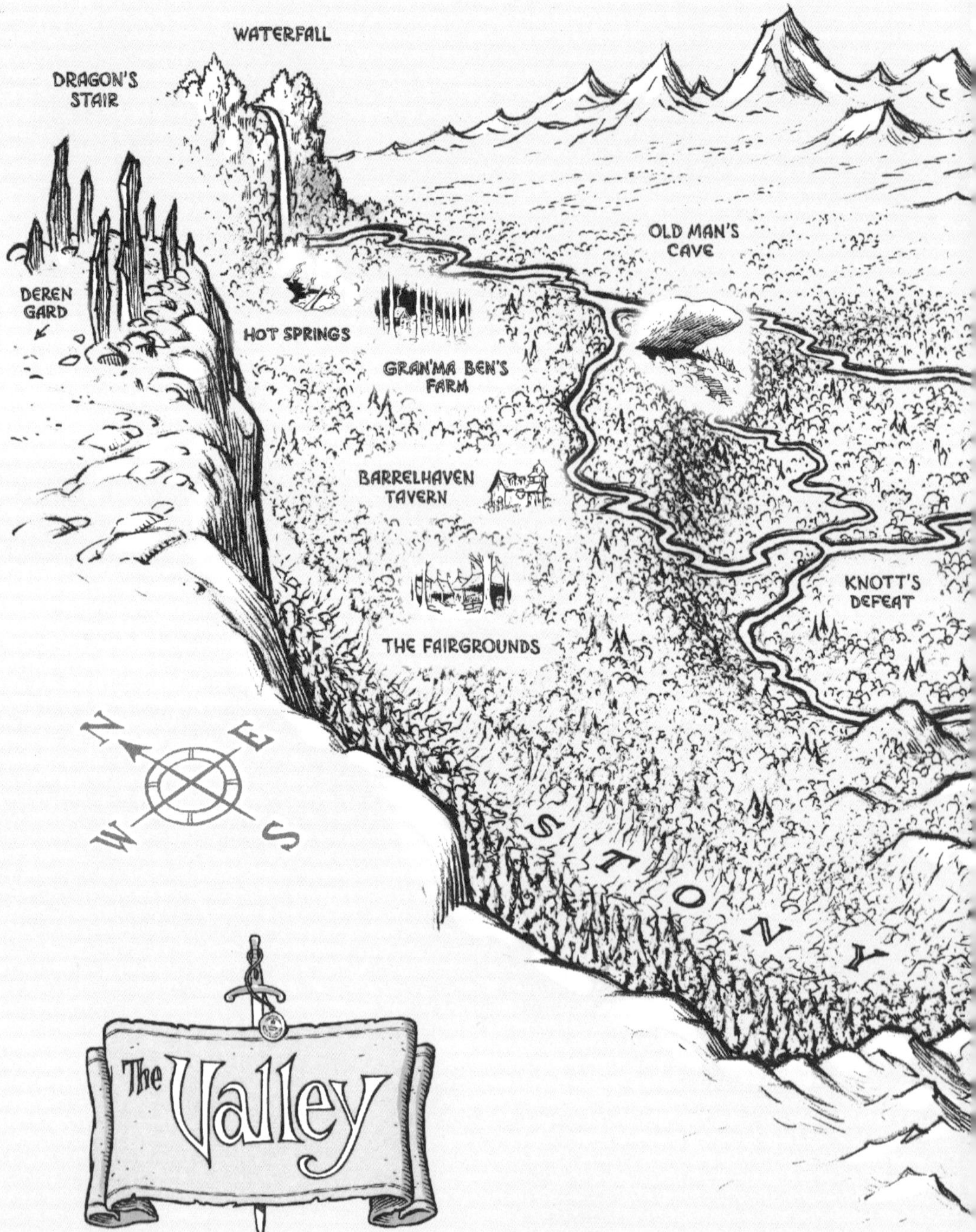
WATERFALL
DRAGON'S STAIR
DEREN GARD
HOT SPRINGS
GRAN'MA BEN'S FARM
OLD MAN'S CAVE
BARRELHAVEN TAVERN
THE FAIRGROUNDS
KNOTT'S DEFEAT
STONY
N
E
S
W
The Valley